The Unbearable Book Club for Unsinkable Girls

JULIE SCHUMACHER

EMBER

Text copyright © 2012 by Julie Schumacher
Cover photograph copyright © 2012 by Ghislain & Marie David de Lossy/Getty Images

All rights reserved. Published in the United States by Ember, an imprint of Random House Children's Books, a division of Random House, Inc., New York. Originally published in hardcover in the United States by Delacorte Press, an imprint of Random House Children's Books, New York, in 2012.

Ember and the E colophon are registered trademarks of Random House, Inc.

Grateful acknowledgement is made to Susan Bergholz Literary Services for permission to reprint excerpts from *The House on Mango Street* by Sandra Cisneros, copyright © 1984 by Sandra Cisneros. All rights reserved. Reprinted by permission of Susan Bergholz Literary Services, New York, NY, and Lamy, NM.

Brief excerpts in this book have been reprinted from the following: *The Left Hand of Darkness* by Ursula K. Le Guin; *Frankenstein* by Mary Shelley; *The Awakening* by Kate Chopin; and "The Yellow Wallpaper" by Charlotte Perkins Gilman.

Visit us on the Web! randomhouse.com/teens
Educators and librarians, for a variety of teaching tools,
visit us at RHTeachersLibrarians.com

The Library of Congress has cataloged the hardcover edition of this work as follows:
Schumacher, Julie.
The Unbearable Book Club for Unsinkable Girls / Julie Schumacher. — 1st ed.
p. cm.
Summary: When four very different small-town Delaware high school girls are forced to join a mother-daughter book club over summer vacation, they end up learning about more than just the books they read.
ISBN 978-0-385-73773-9 (hc) — ISBN 978-0-385-90685-2 (glb)
ISBN 978-0-375-98571-3 (ebook) [1. Books and reading—Fiction.
2. Interpersonal relations—Fiction. 3. Mothers and daughters—Fiction.
4. Book clubs (Discussion groups)—Fiction. 5. Delaware—Fiction.]   I. Title.
PZ7.S3916Un 2012   [Fic]—dc23   2011010266

ISBN 978-0-375-85127-8 (trade pbk.)

RL: 6.5
Printed in the United States of America
10 9 8 7 6 5 4 3 2 1
First Ember Edition 2013

For Bella and Emma and Lawrence Jacobs—
my all-time favorite real-life raucous group

Name: *Adrienne Haus*
Assignment: *Summer Essay*
Instructor: *Ms. Radcliffe*
Class: *English 11 Advanced Placement*

Thesis statement: *Book clubs can kill you. (This essay ends with a person drowning. It turns out you don't need much water for a person to drown.)*

Essay options: Check A or B. Whichever you choose, you must include a bibliography and demonstrate—in your own words—an understanding of at least twenty literary terms listed on the English 11 AP website.
[   ] Option A: argument and analysis
[X] Option B: creative narrative. For example, how have the books you chose to read for this assignment affected you?
Please explain your project in the space below.

I was planning to choose option A because I thought it would be easier. But that was before I dragged myself through the gates of the West New Hope Community Swim Club, before the monster in the closet and the hermaphrodite sex scene and the stolen pills and the revolving blue and red lights of the ambulance and the crazy woman who locked herself away in a yellow room.

I want to apologize for some of the things you'll read in this essay: they might not be appropriate for the assignment. In The Left Hand of Darkness *Genly says, "I'll make my report as if I told a story." That's what I'm going to do. And I'll explain how the books affected me—because whoever I was at the beginning of the summer, I am not that person anymore.*

"The Yellow Wallpaper"

1. SETTING: The place where the author puts the characters. It's like setting a table, except that instead of using plates and silverware, you're using people.

On our first day of membership in what CeeCee would later call the Unbearable Book Club, I was sitting in a plastic lounge chair at the West New Hope, Delaware, community pool, reading a dog-eared copy of "The Yellow Wallpaper." According to the thermometer on the lifeguard stand, it was ninety-seven degrees. My hands were sweating so much they left stains on the pages.

CeeCee paused by the empty recliner next to mine. She was wearing a white crocheted bikini and dark sunglasses, and I saw a copy of "The Yellow Wallpaper" sticking out of her polka-dot bag. CeeCee's thighs didn't touch at the top, I noticed. We weren't friends.

"Don't you think we're too old for this?" she asked.

I wasn't sure she was talking to me: I wasn't the sort of person CeeCee Christiansen usually talked to. The two of us chatting? It was like a dolphin hanging out with a squirrel. "It wasn't my idea," I said as a river of sweat worked its way down my spine. "I think our mothers set it up. They were in a yoga class together."

CeeCee didn't glance in my direction. She unponytailed her long blond hair and let it fall toward the ground like a satin curtain. "Believe me," she said. "It wasn't *my* mother's idea. She doesn't have the imagination."

"Good to know." I wiped my hands on my towel.

Twenty feet from the edges of our chairs, across a stretch of cement too hot to stand on, the pool flashed and glittered, a turquoise rectangle full of multicolored bodies leaping in and out of the water like flying fish.

CeeCee was staring at one of the lifeguards, who was staring back at her and twirling his whistle around his finger on a string: three twirls to the right, three to the left. She had apparently finished talking to me, so I picked up my book.

"You're actually reading it." She sat down and took the cap off a bottle of sunblock. When I turned toward her she smiled a closed-lipped smile, making me think of an alligator sunning itself on a riverbank.

"That's the assignment," I said. "We have to read 'The Yellow Wallpaper' and four other books."

"*And* learn a list of literary terms *and* write an essay," CeeCee said. "This teacher's insane. No one else assigns that kind of homework during the summer. I don't care if it is AP."

I squeegeed the sweat from my eyebrows with an index finger. I didn't mind doing the reading—whatever I read would be more interesting than my day-to-day life—but I wasn't looking forward to the essay. Most of the papers I wrote for school came back with suggestions in the margins about how my ideas could be organized. "I can't find an argument here," my tenth-grade history teacher had said.

"So you're not going to read the books?" I asked CeeCee. I didn't know Ms. Radcliffe yet, but she had a reputation for being stern and precise. I imagined her snapping a steel-edged ruler on my desk.

"It doesn't matter if you read them." CeeCee squirted a white ribbon of lotion onto her stomach. "Most of the books we read for school are crap. I usually just read the summary online, or I read the first couple of pages and then skip to the end." She glanced at my copy of "The Yellow Wallpaper." "You're planning to read the whole thing?"

"I think that's the point of a book," I said. "You start at the beginning and you read to the end." I hadn't learned how to read until halfway through first grade, and I still felt grateful to my teacher, Ms. Hampl, who had knelt by my desk one afternoon and smoothed her finger across the parallel rows of two-dimensional black marks in my book—and as if she had opened a hidden door, I felt the patterned surface break and give way, and the words let me in. I still loved opening a book and feeling like I was physically entering the page, the ordinary world fizzing and blurring around the edges until it disappeared.

"You don't have to take Advanced Placement," I pointed out.

"Right. Only the helpless take regular English."

5

CeeCee squeezed some lotion onto her arms, which were thin and hairless. "AP classes have two kinds of kids in them: the kids who are smart, and the kids who don't want to spend the year in a room full of losers. Do you have a four-oh?"

"A four-oh grade average? No." I wasn't sure what my average was. Teachers often referred to me as a student with "a lot of potential." This meant they *expected* me to be smart; but in fact my mind was often packing a mental suitcase and wandering off on its own. I sometimes pictured all the things I had learned during the previous week at school jumping into brightly painted railroad cars and disappearing into the distance on a speeding train.

CeeCee scanned the perimeter of the pool, presumably for more-worthwhile people to talk to. The pickings were slim. "So what's your deal?" she asked. "I don't really know you. Who are you supposed to be?"

Who was I *supposed* to be? I was Adrienne Haus. I was fifteen. I lived in West New Hope with my mother, who had signed me up for a summer book club. Now I was reading—or trying to read—a book at the pool.

CeeCee recapped her lotion. "Are you a religious freak?" she asked.

"No."

"A shoplifter?"

"No."

"A partier?"

"No." I was waiting for her to come up with something else. "Are those my only choices?"

"Those are three of them." She picked up her cell

phone and frowned at its screen. "You'd look better if you parted your hair on the other side. Why do you have that thing on your leg?"

One of the lifeguards, his calves dangling like dark, hairy fruit from the perch of his chair, blew his whistle at a cluster of boys who were holding each other's heads underwater.

"It's a knee brace," I said.

"Can't you take it off?" CeeCee asked. "It's going to stink."

"I don't think it stinks." I sniffed at the thick black cloth on my leg, then gently unfastened its Velcro straps and looked at my knee: it was swollen and fleshy, like an unidentified vegetable discovered at the bottom of a bin. "I fractured my kneecap," I said, talking more to myself than to CeeCee. "And tore my ACL. I'm supposed to exercise my leg in the water."

I expected CeeCee to be disgusted by the sight of my scar—a pink wrinkled worm—but she lifted her sunglasses and leaned toward me for a better look.

"You probably heard about it at school," I said. "An ambulance came for me after lunch." I explained to CeeCee that about a week before the end of the school year, I had tripped over nothing in a crowded stairwell, and even before my knee hit the metal riser I understood that the six-week canoe trip I had signed up for with my best friend, Liz, was going to happen without me and I would be stuck in West New Hope, alone. "Liz left last weekend," I said. "I saved four hundred dollars toward that trip." Liz was probably paddling across the Canadian border on her way to being friends with someone else. "Anyway," I said. "You probably knew most of that already."

"Actually, no," CeeCee said. "I know nothing about you. You're like an Etch A Sketch to me. Or a dry-erase board. You know: blank."

"Thanks," I said.

She crossed her legs and waved halfheartedly to someone on the other side of the diving board. "It is a coincidence, though," she said. "I'm not supposed to be here, either. I should be in France. My sister's studying there, for the year. But my parents canceled my trip because I dented their car. *One* of their cars. They got all freaked out because I don't have a license."

"You have a permit?" I asked.

A little boy wearing dinosaur swim trunks paused by our chairs.

"Not yet. Anyway, as punishment," CeeCee said, "because I was such an 'irresponsible girl,' the parentals signed me up for summer school. Apparently, sitting in an unair-conditioned classroom with Monsieur Crowne every day for six weeks is the perfect way to learn French. It's much better than spending the summer in Paris. I don't like little kids," she said to the boy in the dinosaur trunks. He wandered away.

With her phone, CeeCee took a picture of her painted toenails in front of the pool. "When I think about being stuck in West New Hope in a literary play group with my mother I want to scoop my eyeballs out with a spoon," she said. "This town is hell during the summer. There's nobody here."

8

I knew what she meant. The only things to do in town involved the pool and a Softee Freeze and a decrepit mini-putt and a handful of unpopular stores in the badly spelled Towne Centre. The joke about West New Hope was that there was no East New Hope, and there was *No Hope.* We lived in a flat, oversized suburb west of nothing, a dot on the map in a state people drove through to get somewhere else.

Besides, most of the people our age who had hung around during previous summers had gotten jobs (all of which were taken by the time I applied, with my leg in a brace), or had left town to do something fulfilling and educational: they were working in orphanages or curing diseases or preventing war. My plan for the summer? Relax, read, and spend some unstructured leisure time not being at school.

I looked around the pool for people over the age of twelve and under thirty. "There's Jill D'Amato. She's in our book club." I pointed. Past the lifeguard stand and the shuffleboard court and the baby pool, between the men's and women's locker rooms (a series of dripping cinder-block caverns that always smelled of Band-Aids and feet), Jill was working the snack bar. She sat in a folding chair under an awning, selling Italian water ice and soda and chips and ice cream. When I'd walked past her earlier, she was reading an SAT prep book and a thesaurus. Jill's mother had also attended the infamous yoga class that spawned the idea of the mother-daughter book club of No Hope, DE.

"Oh, good God," CeeCee said. "I know that girl. She

was in choir with me last year. She likes country music. And she's sitting there studying. Bizarre. Is she a friend of yours?"

"Not really."

Jill looked up as if she had heard us.

"So who do you usually hang out with?" CeeCee asked.

"Usually . . . Liz," I said, adjusting the top of my bathing suit, which appeared to be losing its elastic. "Liz Zerendow. But she's—"

"Gone for the summer," CeeCee finished. "I already heard."

I didn't bother to ask her who she was friends with because the answer was obvious: the ruling class of glamorous despots who floated like rare and colorful aquatic creatures through the toxic fishbowl that was our school. My general goal—and it appeared to have succeeded—was to remain forever undetectable to their radar.

CeeCee seemed to have temporarily run out of questions. I leaned back in my chair. The heat was barbaric. The sky, cloudless and flat, was pressing down on us like a steam iron. I shut my eyes and slipped into a coma for a little while, dreaming about Liz paddling away in a silver canoe on a strand of blue water.

I woke up when the lifeguards blared their whistles. They called for a buddy check—CeeCee lightly touched my wrist and said "Check"—followed by fifteen minutes of adult swim.

I rubbed my eyes and sat up and found my place in "The Yellow Wallpaper." The story was strange, but I liked it. It was about a woman who was depressed and whose husband thought she would feel better if they rented a house in the middle of nowhere so she could spend all her time doing nothing in a yellow room.

I am glad my case is not serious! But these nervous troubles are dreadfully depressing. John does not know how much I really suffer.

"Are you ignoring me?" CeeCee asked. "I *said*, why did you agree?"

"Why did I agree to what?" I tugged at my bathing suit again. Bathing suits never seemed to look good on me. My body was thick in the middle, almost cylindrical. The word *trunk*—as in trees and elephants—often sprang unfortunately to mind.

"Why did you agree to be in the book club?" CeeCee watched me struggle with my bathing suit. "You said it wasn't your idea."

I noticed the waterfall of her hair and the silver rings on three of her fingers and her hip bones poking out on either side of the perfect flat plane of her golden stomach. "I burned our house down," I said. "I had a choice between book club and jail."

CeeCee turned her head slowly and looked straight at me for the first time. "That was funny," she said. "Unless you think you're making fun of me."

I went back to my book.

Nobody would believe what an effort it is to do what little I am able—to dress and entertain, and order things.

11

"I wouldn't mind as much if it was a *father*-daughter book club," CeeCee said. "Fathers aren't as annoying." She popped the top on a can of soda. "Are your parentals fairly normal?"

"I just have a mom," I said, still looking at my book. "I don't have a dad."

"Cool. He's dead?" CeeCee sipped from her drink.

"No. He's just not around."

"So he ran off? Is he a deadbeat?"

"I never met him. He's not . . . part of the picture." I went back to the yellow room and the gate at the stairs and the bars on the windows.

John has cautioned me not to give way to fancy in the least.
He says that with my imaginative power and habit of
story-making, a nervous weakness like mine is sure to lead to
all manner of excited fancies—

"I bet you think about him subconsciously."

"What?" The noise and splashing and heat and commotion filtered into my brain; I pulled the book closer.

He says that with my imaginative power and habit of
story-making, a nervous weakness like mine—

"That's probably why you couldn't answer my question."

. . . a nervous weakness like mine is sure to lead to—

CeeCee pressed her icy can of soda against my arm. The yellow room fizzled and disappeared. "What question?" I asked.

"About what kind of person you are," she said. "You couldn't tell me and now I'm curious. You couldn't even describe yourself. Don't you think that's"—she glanced at my knee—"lame?"

"Why are you talking to me?" I asked.

CeeCee tipped back her head and finished her soda. "This chair was empty. I saw the book in your hands. You could say that literature brought us together. Also, I felt like messing with your head."

"Thanks."

"You're extremely welcome," she said, and for the first time since she had sat down, I didn't dislike her.

Another blast from the whistle. Adult swim was over. CeeCee stood up and stretched. "Time to get in the water. Are you coming?"

I told her I'd rather stay in my chair and finish the book. "There are too many people in the pool right now."

"There are always too many people in the pool," CeeCee said. She tied her hair into a perfect golden knot. "The water's just a big tub of chlorine full of skin flakes and gobs of hair and snot and bacteria. But you can't let that stop you."

I hesitated. "I don't want anyone bumping into me," I said. "My leg's really sore."

CeeCee was poised at the lip of the pool. "You said you're supposed to be exercising. I'll run interference for you." She hopped in, holding her elbows above the surface. The water was full of little kids diving for pennies and swimming through each other's legs. She turned to face me. "Jump to Mommy."

Different moments in my life remind me of books. Looking at CeeCee holding her arms out in front of her, I thought about Heidi coaxing Clara to walk. I limped to the stairs and took hold of the handrail. Two little boys came churning toward me, thrashing their limbs.

CeeCee grabbed the nearer kid by the ankle. "Out of my way," she said, "or I crush you." She turned him around and launched him like a boat in the other direction. "Let's go, Grandma." I walked down the stairs, the water a cool blue bandage against my leg.

Liz was probably swimming in a lake somewhere. She was taking AP English, too. She was planning to read the books in the tent the two of us were supposed to have shared. She would probably write the entire essay in an afternoon—Liz was a model of efficiency—when she got back.

"Why is that strange little person staring at you?" CeeCee asked. She created a narrow lane at the edge of the pool, where I paced back and forth.

"What strange little person?" I wiped the chlorine out of my eyes. Behind our recliners, on the other side of the diamond-chain-link fence, was a scrawny girl wearing oversized shorts and a shirt and sneakers.

"That's Wallis," I said. She was the final daughter in the mother-daughter book club. Unlike CeeCee and Jill and me, Wallis had apparently found out about the group and asked to be included.

"Is she . . . in special ed?" CeeCee asked.

"No. She skipped a grade," I said. "It might have been two."

"Unsettling. Why is she *outside* the fence?" CeeCee shaded her eyes. "It's a hundred degrees. And isn't Wallace a guy's name?"

"No, it's spelled *W-A-L-L-I-S*," I said. "She was in my history class last term. She moved here in January and made a speech on her first day, telling everyone in the room that she was named for the woman who was supposed to be the queen of England."

"Do you mean Elizabeth?"

"No. Elizabeth *is* the queen," I said.

Wallis had turned away from us and was shuffling through the uncut grass between the parking lot and the locker rooms. She had a book with her. I didn't have to see its cover to know what it was: "The Yellow Wallpaper."

CeeCee stiff-armed a little girl wearing orange floaters out of our way.

"Do you want me to tell you what the book's about?" I asked.

CeeCee shrugged. "Don't worry about it."

I paused at the edge of the pool, where a filter was sucking and spitting out water like a plastic mouth. "It's set about a hundred years ago," I said. "The main character, the protagonist, is a wealthy woman who's depressed. She has a baby, and—"

15

"Did you say 'protagonist'?" CeeCee asked. "Are you deliberately using the words on that literary terms list?"

I noticed that Jill, beneath the awning above the snack bar, was staring at us. "I'm not using them *deliberately*," I said. I tried to ignore a stabbing feeling at the base of my knee. "Anyway, the woman is married to a doctor who spends all his time hovering over her and making her rest in a yellow room. Whenever she looks at the wallpaper—"

"You don't have to tell me the end," CeeCee said. She caught a dead bug in her hands and threw it out of the pool. "I read that part already."

Wallis shuffled past the pool's main entrance, still outside the fence, head down and reading. She didn't stop to buy a ticket or a summer pass.

"So you read the end but not the beginning?"

"Yeah. There are a couple of lines in the last few pages that made me laugh."

I tried to imagine which parts of a story about a person losing her mind would be funny.

"Hang on." CeeCee swam to the ladder and climbed out and flipped through the book. "Here it is. The 'protagonist' keeps telling her husband that she feels like crap but he doesn't believe her. He calls her a 'blessed little goose.' And when she says she wants to get out of the yellow room because it's making her sick"—CeeCee tossed the book back onto her chair—"her husband says, 'Bless her little heart. She shall be as sick as she pleases.'"

I pulled myself to the ladder and got out, feeling thousands of drops of water chatter and prickle against my skin. The cement cooked my feet.

"'She shall be as sick as she pleases,'" CeeCee sang. "You don't think that's hilarious?"

I shrugged. Having done nothing all day, I was exhausted. Lying down on the plastic slats of my recliner, I closed my eyes and tried to imagine the scene from above: a flat green park, a silver fence with one scrawny girl positioned outside it, and set in the center, like a gaudy gem in a ring, the shimmering turquoise body of the pool.

I listened to the *whap-ap-ap-ap-ap* of the diving board. "This heat could kill a person," I said.

"Blessed little goose," CeeCee said. "I wonder who it will be."

• • • • • • • • • • • • •

2. METAPHOR and SIMILE: A metaphor is a fancy way of describing something by comparing it to something else. Instead of saying, "He has bad breath," you could say, "His mouth is a fiery pit of odorous garbage." A simile is the same thing but you use *like* or *as*. So you would say, "His mouth is *like* a fiery pit of odorous garbage."

"How would you describe me?" I asked. "If we weren't related."

It was Sunday, our first book club day, and my mother and I were in the front yard, weeding the lawn. This was a completely pointless activity: my mother refused to use pesticides, so most of what was green in the lawn needed pulling.

"How would I describe you to whom?" my mother asked. My mother is the sort of person who uses the word *whom*. She teaches English to immigrants, mostly adults.

"You answered my question with a question," I said,

"which probably means you're stalling for time. Which means you think I'm not describable."

"Would that be good or bad, if you were indescribable?" My mother tossed a dandelion into the plastic bucket between us. I was in charge of removing tangled networks of creeping Charlie with a tool that looked like a witch's hand, while my mother was extracting—with a big two-pronged metal fork—the rat-tail roots of dandelions.

"Probably bad," I said, remembering my conversation at the pool with CeeCee. "Other people can be described." I thought about a phrase I had read somewhere—"neither fish nor fowl." *That sounds like me.*

"If you want a description," my mother said, "I'd be happy to describe you."

"Okay," I said.

My mother moved on to a new crop of weeds. "I'd definitely describe you as imaginative," she said. "A little absentminded. And certainly impressionable."

"What do you mean, 'impressionable'?"

"*Impressionable* means . . . susceptible. Open to influence," my mother said.

"I know what the word *means*," I told her.

She sat back on her heels. "When you were younger you used to act out parts from the books you liked. Do you remember? For weeks you followed me around and finger-spelled into my hands because you were pretending to be Helen Keller."

"That makes me sound like an idiot," I said. But I remembered the Helen Keller phase. And I suddenly wanted

19

to shut my eyes and put on a pair of sound-canceling headphones and plunge my hand in a stream of cool W-A-T-E-R.

"And I think you're amusing and good-natured—most of the time," my mother said. "You're fairly independent. Easygoing. How's that?"

"That's it?" I asked. *"Impressionable? Easygoing?"* She might as well have looked up *bland* in a thesaurus. *Easygoing* described the interchangeable roster of strangers who delivered our mail.

"How would you characterize yourself?" my mother said. She plunged her metal fork into the ground.

This was the same question CeeCee had asked me. It reminded me of my discovery, a few years earlier, that at the beginning of a lot of books, there's a Library of Congress classification. It might say *World War II, biography* or *Elephants, fiction.* It made me wish that the Librarian of Congress, whoever he was, would make some categories like that for me:

Haus, Adrienne. 1. People with knee ailments—
Biography. 2. Bored fifteen-year-old Delawareans—
Nonfiction. 3. People without hobbies who have only
one friend, and that friend is away for the summer.
4. People who have never met their fathers.

But I seemed to be a person without a category. I was *impressionable.* Easily molded, average, shapeless. When I opened my closet door in the morning and looked in the mirror, I almost expected to see a paramecium wearing a wig. *Who are you supposed to be?*

"Do you think I should part my hair on the other side?" I asked.

"I don't know," my mother said. "Would that make you look different?"

"It might." I had a low and irregular forehead. Even Liz had once told me I had the hairline of an australopithecine. I swept my bangs from right to left, but they immediately flopped back into place as if to say, *Don't joke around; we live over here.*

My mother wiped the sweat from her neck. It was hot again. Every day it was hot, as if the weather had been imported from a place where people sewed palm leaves together and used them for clothing. "How's your knee?" she asked. "Have you been doing your physical therapy?"

"Yes, on land and at sea," I said. "I walked through the pool the other day. It was very exciting."

My mother sighed. "I'm sorry you couldn't go on your canoe trip. I've probably said that already. I know it's a terrible disappointment."

Of course she was right. It was a disappointment. But it occurred to me, maybe because she'd mentioned it several times, that my mother was at least as disappointed as I was. She had bought me a new sleeping bag and a backpack and hiking boots (she had managed to return everything except the boots) and had been looking forward to seeing me off for the entire summer. She had probably imagined that after forty days of wilderness adventure (followed by a week at Liz's grandparents' farm in Minnesota) I was going to return to West New Hope fit and decisive, like Ernest Shackleton or Admiral Peary. My mother believed in goals and projects and self-improvement. She might have thought the trip would improve me. She might have wanted me to be improved.

I adjusted my brace. Maybe CeeCee was right about the smell. I detected a subtle mix of eggshell and roadkill and pee.

"What time are they coming tonight?" I asked.

"Seven-thirty. Did you finish the book?"

"Twice," I said. "It was only around thirty pages."

I don't know why I should write this, wrote the woman in the yellow room. *I don't want to. I don't feel able.*

Feeling limp, I lay down on the lawn. "Just so you're warned ahead of time," I said, "this book club is probably going to be a disaster."

"Why's that?" My mother speared another dandelion.

"Because, first of all, fifteen is too old to be in a mother-daughter book club. Second of all, the thing about books? They're made for one person at a time. That's why they're small. You can hold them in your hand. Movies are made for groups of people. It's a different thing."

My mother thanked me for this explanation and said that we didn't have to read simultaneously; the book club was based, instead, on discussion.

"And third of all," I said, "Wallis and Jill and CeeCee and I are too different. We're not the same types of people."

"Wouldn't that make the meetings more interesting?" my mother asked.

22

"Actually, no." I rolled onto my stomach. Deep in the grass, a group of caramel-colored ants was migrating from one ant village to another, probably carrying ant-sized tables, chairs, dishes, pillows, and lamps into their tiny homes. "You'd have to be sentenced to high school all over again to understand it," I said, "but you can't force people my age to talk to each other. Bad things will happen."

"Why are you staring at the ground like that?" my mother asked. She tugged the bucket of weeds across one of the anthills, wiping out half a civilization. "The book club's not permanent," she said. "It's just for the summer—once a week—and it'll give you a chance to widen your social circle."

This was my mother's tactful way of pointing out that, since Liz was in Canada and every other able-bodied person in town was gainfully employed, I would probably be spending most of my summer alone. Liz and I had been best friends for six years. She had earned my eternal affection at the end of fourth grade by intercepting a series of scribbled insults directed toward me by Billy Secor. She had opened the crumpled sheet of paper and read it, then put the entire thing in her mouth and chewed and swallowed it, saying only that Billy had spelled *retarded* "redarded."

"People my age don't have 'social circles.'" I sat up, hauling my leg behind me like a suitcase. "And I don't want to have 'story time' with these other girls. I barely know them."

"You'll get to know them," my mother said. "That's what happens when you spend time with people. It's good to be social."

"Hm," I said. I watched as the neighbors' cat, Mr. Finkle, his orange belly nearly touching the ground, carried a chipmunk along the sidewalk in his yellow teeth. The chipmunk was obviously dead, and Mr. Finkle, swaying side to side, somehow managed to look mournful about it. He ambled slowly across the sidewalk, our local Charon, a furry ferryboat king.

"Are you weeding or daydreaming over there?" my mother asked.

I pulled up a cluster of creeping Charlie as thick as a bath mat and threw it, Frisbee-style, into the bucket. I felt sticky and restless. *There is something absent in me,* I thought. *Something incomplete.* Even my mother couldn't describe me. There was something empty in me that in other people was full.

"Do you think it screwed me up that I never met my father?" I asked.

My mother stopped weeding and turned to face me. "Where did that come from? Do you think you're screwed up?"

"Not necessarily," I said. A beetle crawled toward me, its blue-gray body like a metal toy lost in the grass. "But maybe that's why I'm not describable. I never met my father but I might take after him. Maybe it's his fault that I'm clumsy and average and boring and bland."

"I didn't realize that you were clumsy and average and boring and bland," my mother said.

Mr. Finkle tenderly positioned the departed chipmunk on a bed of grass in the shade of the house. His usual pattern was to devour the body, then deposit the head—with

24

its terrified milky-white eyeballs—next to the driver's-side door of my mother's car.

"Do you think I'd have turned out different if I had two parents?" I asked.

"Of course you would have. And you'd have turned out different*ly* if you had three parents. Is there a reason you're bringing this up? Something you want to ask?"

We hadn't talked about my nonexistent father for a while. My mother had always been honest about him. If he'd known about me, she always said, he would have loved me. But my mother had no idea where he lived and didn't know his last name. When I got older and asked her more specific questions, she told me that her (very brief) relationship with my father was "consensual"—but that he wasn't a boyfriend. She also assured me that I wasn't an "accident." She was twenty-eight when I was born. "And if I had decided I didn't want a baby, you wouldn't be here," she said.

I cleaned some dirt from my fingernails. My mother's policy about father-related questions was clear and consistent: she would answer any question at all, at any time—but she would not *over*answer. I suspected she had taken this question-and-answer idea from a parenting book.

"It's not like I spend a lot of time thinking about him," I said.

My mother was waiting, but I wasn't sure what to ask her. When I was little, I mainly wanted to know what my father looked like. Given my own indefinite shape, I wanted to know if he was fat. (She said he wasn't.) For a while I pictured him as Professor Bhaer from *Little Women*: a roundish, full-bearded man whose pockets had holes in them. Later, I imagined him as Herman E. Calloway from *Bud, Not Buddy,* and then as Sergeant Flannigan from *Mrs. Mike.*

My mother shaded her eyes. "What's that cat doing over there? He'd better not be heading toward my car."

"He is," I said. "And he's got a severed head in his mouth. He wants you to add it to the collection." Mr. Finkle glanced sadly toward us, then meandered across the driveway, clasping his prize. "What if it turns out I'm related to a psychopath?" I asked. "Or a serial killer?"

My mother seemed to consider this possibility. "Do you feel you have psychopathic blood in your veins?"

I looked down at my forearms, where a couple of bluish veins were visible. "I don't have the energy to be a murderer," I said.

"And you feel queasy at the sight of blood," my mother added. "Which would be a deterrent."

I picked up the witch's hand again. "I just want to be . . . interesting," I said. "And don't tell me *you* think I'm interesting. That doesn't count. You have to be interested in me, because you're my mother."

"What? I'm sorry," my mother said. "Did you say something? I might have dozed off."

"Ha ha," I said. "I'm trying to have a serious conversation here. I don't know if you've noticed, but I'm almost an adult." I paused. "If you died—if you were hit by a bus— would I still have to live with Aunt Beatrice?"

Aunt Beatrice was my mother's sister, who lived in Atlanta.

26

"I suppose, now that you're 'almost an adult,' you'd have the option of moving in with Liz," my mother said. "We could talk to her parents."

"Okay." I scratched at the ground with the witch's fingers. "That would probably be better: you don't get along all that well with Aunt Beatrice."

"I wouldn't have to get along with her. I'd be squashed by the bus, remember?" She tapped the back of my wrist. "You don't need to claw at the ground like that."

"Oh. Sorry." I looked at the patch of earth between us: it was nearly bare, with narrow fingermarks streaking the dirt.

My mother went back to her dandelions. "Is there anything else you want to ask, while we're having our Serious Adult Conversation?"

Several questions jostled for position in my brain.

1) Why did my mother always answer my questions with a question?
2) Why did I feel like half a person sometimes?
3) What kind of wacky nine-year-old liked to pretend to be Helen Keller?

"What other books are we going to read?" I asked. "I mean, in this book club."

"We'll have to choose from Ms. Radcliffe's list," my mother said. "Maybe we should stick to books by women. That would narrow it down."

The tiny, fictional Ms. Radcliffe who lived in my brain snapped her metal ruler. "Are we almost done out here?" I

27

asked. Our lawn was small, but we seemed to have weeded only about two percent of it.

"Five more minutes," my mother said. "And I think you should give this book club a chance. What terrible things could possibly happen just because a group of mothers and daughters decided to get together to talk about books?"

"I don't know yet," I said.

Mr. Finkle's golden hindquarters flashed in the bushes.

"It's good to interact with people you wouldn't ordinarily talk to, and read books you wouldn't ordinarily read. Be open-minded. Be willing to experiment. That's my advice." My mother wiped her forehead and said it was impossible that the entire summer was going to be this hot.

She was wrong about the heat.

And she would come to regret her advice to me as well.

3. CHARACTERS: The people in a novel or story. In this essay I guess the main characters are CeeCee and Jill and Wallis and me. And maybe my mother, who would be offended if I left her out.

Unlike CeeCee, who didn't seem to enjoy reading, Jill D'Amato was the sort of person you'd expect to find in a book club. At school she was the queen of extra-curriculars: the catcher on the softball team, the assistant editor of the yearbook, a member of Debate Club (I had heard her give an animal rights presentation in the school cafeteria), and apparently a fan of country music. Even when she was obviously wrong, Jill assumed she was right. When she and her mother showed up for book club fifteen minutes earlier than anyone else, Jill insisted that my mother and I had made a mistake about the time. "It was definitely seven-fifteen," she said.

Then she followed me into the kitchen and gave me a Coming Attractions summary of the rest of her life, which was all planned out: she would go to the University of Delaware for college, join a sorority, and become a nurse. After she graduated, she was going to adopt a greyhound, and she wasn't going to get married until she'd had a good job for at least two years.

Jill had a way of inhaling before she talked, sucking the air through her nose. "Nursing is a great profession," she said while I searched for a can of lemonade. "You don't have to work in a hospital. You can do home care or private practice, or you can work in a nursing home or do research. There are a lot of different possibilities."

"Sounds like you've got it all worked out." I burrowed into the freezer—a wasteland of shattered pie shells, half-empty ice cream containers, runaway coffee beans, and ancient hamburgers dressed up in thick frosted jackets. "But why don't you want to be a doctor?"

She inhaled through her nostrils. "Why would I want to be a doctor?"

"I don't know. Because they make more money?" I plucked a can of frozen pink lemonade from underneath a package of peas. "It seems kind of weird that you've already made those kinds of decisions."

"I don't think it's weird," Jill said. "What do you want to be?"

"I don't know." I remembered the rhyme my mother used to recite when I was little: *Rich man, poor man, beggar man, thief; doctor, lawyer, Indian chief. Tinker, tailor, soldier, sailor, gentleman, apothecary—out go you.* But wasn't that a rhyme about who you would marry? And what the heck was a tinker? "I definitely don't want to be a nurse."

Jill tossed an ice cube into the pink cave of her mouth. I could tell she was irritated with me; but she didn't have to listen to the air whistling into my nose. "I've been wondering why you invited me here," she said.

"I didn't invite you." I rinsed out a pitcher; there were several dead fruit flies inside it. "No offense," I said. "I didn't invite anyone." Remembering my mother's advice about being open-minded and friendly, I shared my current theory: that we might as well have started a reading group with the Virgin Mary, Abraham Lincoln, Oprah Winfrey, and Genghis Khan.

"Okay. Then I know who Genghis is," Jill said. "I saw her this afternoon coming out of the drugstore, wearing a tiny white skirt and yellow sandals. You were at the pool with her. What do you think she weighs?"

"You want to know what CeeCee weighs?" I asked. "I haven't weighed her."

"Probably one-oh-five. I'm good at estimating," Jill said. "I weigh one thirty-five. You probably weigh, what: one fifty? One fifty-five?"

I looked at the clock: *Only two more hours*, I thought, *and this first unfortunate evening will be over.*

Jill tossed another ice cube into her mouth. Her face was round and tan and smooth, her skin the color of a light brown egg. "What I heard about CeeCee," she said, "in case you're interested, is that her parents have forced her to be in the book club. Which means you and Wallis and I are her punishment."

"That's a nice way of looking at it," I said. "We're like a penal colony, with books."

Jill pulled her thick black hair into a ponytail. "I'm just agreeing with what you said earlier. We're not a typical group. Wallis is a miniature prodigy, and I'm into sports, and you—" Jill looked me quickly up and down. "You've screwed up your leg or whatever. But CeeCee's different. She's . . ."

"What?" I dumped the lemonade—*plop*—into the plastic pitcher.

"I'm trying to think of the word," Jill said. "*Ominous?* I've been doing flash cards, getting ready for the PSAT. Are you going to sign up for the SAT prep class this fall?"

"I don't think you can use *ominous* for people," I said. "That doesn't make sense."

"It makes sense for CeeCee," Jill said.

The doorbell rang.

"Adrienne, would you get that?" my mother called.

"Hang on," I yelled. I mixed the lemonade with water.

Jill lingered next to me at the sink. "Why do you think CeeCee was hanging out with you at the pool?"

"It was only for a couple of hours," I said. Was the idea of someone spending time with me suspicious?

The doorbell rang again: *ba-DANG-ba-DUM*. "Adrienne?" my mother called.

"Go ahead. It's probably her," Jill said. "My theory? CeeCee thinks you're going to be easy to push around."

Because my mother didn't believe in using the air conditioner even though we had one, the first meeting of the Mother-Daughter Literary Punishment Group was held out on the porch. Our house was small: two narrow bed-rooms, a kitchen, a TV room/den, and a long book-filled hallway my mother referred to as "the cattle chute." The screen porch, surrounded by lilacs that shaded and per-fumed it, was the only space we had for "entertaining." It stuck out from the back of our little blue house like an afterthought.

Jill's mother, Glory, who had a bubbly, exaggerated way of speaking, was effervescing about the snacks my mother had assembled: a plate of celery and carrots, some warped-looking breadsticks, and a sagging block of cheese that smelled like the inside of a sweat-stained shoe.

"We're waiting for two more people," my mother said. She asked if anyone had read anything interesting lately.

Jill had just read *The Lovely Bones*. Her mother had read something frightening (she couldn't remember the title) by Stephen King. CeeCee's mother, Dana, who looked like an older and more expensive version of CeeCee, was halfway through Darwin's *On the Origin of Species*—because that was what CeeCee had told her the book club had decided to read.

My mother said that no matter which books we chose, she could probably find copies for us at the community col-lege library because of her job.

I put Ms. Radcliffe's list on the table, next to the cheese. Judging from the number of books she listed as "college preparatory—highly recommended," she was going to work us hard all year. Still, I thought, she would have to be better than Mrs. Dierks, the other English 11 teacher. Mrs.

Dierks was famous for keeping a cot and a pillow in her classroom, because (she claimed) her students' opinions exhausted her to the point where she had to lie down.

The first embarrassing moment of the book club: my mother felt inspired to make a speech about my literary habits. "Adrienne doesn't read fast," she said. "But she truly immerses herself in a book."

"That's right. I read deep," I said. Then I looked at my mother. *Please don't tell them about Helen Keller.*

"CeeCee used to read almost every day when she was younger." CeeCee's mother, a collection of thick gold bracelets clinking gracefully around one of her wrists, reached for my copy of "The Yellow Wallpaper." "I used to take her to the library once a week and get her a big stack of books. But even in elementary school her social life began to take the place of reading. I suppose that happens."

CeeCee had been adjusting the speed on a portable fan with her toes. But as soon as her mother spoke, she went still, as if a tiny electric current had run up her spine. "I hate it when you do that," she said.

Jill's mother smiled and said she hadn't heard of some of the books on the list. Where was *Little Women*? Where were *Sounder* and *Where the Red Fern Grows*?

"You hate it when I do what?" CeeCee's mother asked.

"When you talk about me like I'm not even here." CeeCee reached for the carrots. "Or like I'm some kind of pet."

Her mother brushed a crumb from her lap, sending a

cascade of bracelets tinkling down the length of her arm. "A pet?" she asked.

"You start talking to somebody else's parent, and then you point at me"—CeeCee gestured toward her mother with a carrot stick—"and you say, 'We're having such trouble with ours these days. Just look at her over there: she's such a problem. I wish she wouldn't poop in the yard.'"

"I didn't know you were pooping in the yard," her mother said. "You should have told me."

"Mine's acting surly today," CeeCee went on. "And she doesn't eat. I think she's bulimic." She chewed up a carrot, then opened her mouth and caught the slimy orange debris in a napkin. She turned to Jill's mother, who seemed both confused and fascinated, as if she were watching a play and had begun to realize she was in the wrong theater.

"Does yours do that?" CeeCee asked.

Behind them, the screen door creaked open. Wallis had crossed the sea of dry grass at the back of the house, and stood on the bristly welcome mat with a sleeve of crackers in her hand. "I'm here for the book club," she said.

The six of us turned toward her. Wallis wore thick black plastic glasses and a button-down shirt and loose khaki shorts like an archaeologist's. She had a buzzing monotone of a voice, scratchy and low. If a bear could be trained to talk, I thought, it would sound like Wallis.

My mother opened the door and thanked her for the crackers.

"My mother couldn't come tonight," Wallis said, stepping onto the porch. "She's working on something and said we should go ahead without her. She sends regrets." Wallis blinked and looked at each of us, her face washed clean of all human expression, and then sat next to me. She clutched a library copy of "The Yellow Wallpaper" in her hands.

Our order of business: to discuss book number one, which every student in Ms. Radcliffe's class had to read, and then decide—in consultation with the AP English list—on our next four choices.

"Whatever we decide to read should be short," Jill said. "Some of us are working this summer. At least one of us is."

Jill's mother added that it was important that we consider diversity.

We all looked at Jill. She was adopted and Chinese; her parents were white.

My mother suggested that we could narrow our choices by limiting ourselves to books written by women. "*Pride and Prejudice* is on the list," she said.

Wallis asked whether we were limiting ourselves to novels or if we could also include nonfiction.

"I always loved *Black Beauty*," Jill's mother gushed.

"Animal cruelty is always inspiring," CeeCee agreed. "But I don't think *Black Beauty* counts as nonfiction, unless the horse wrote it."

My mother suggested *Pride and Prejudice* again.

"You've already read that," I said. "You've probably read it a dozen times." My mother was obsessed with Jane Austen. Only a few hundred years kept her and Jane from being friends.

Finally we decided that, based on the list, each of us would write down the titles of four different books—written by women—that we wanted to read.

In the meantime, in an effort to discuss "The Yellow Wallpaper," we veered into a meandering conversation about Vincent van Gogh and his missing ear, then listened to Jill tell a story (she claimed it was true) about a woman with some sort of dream disorder who had chewed through a wooden bedpost in her sleep.

Anyone who gnawed through a wooden bedpost, CeeCee said, probably deserved to be locked in a yellow room.

"Adrienne?" Jill's mother asked. "You've been quiet over there. What did you think of the book?"

I looked at the paperback in my hand. I found it almost impossible, after I'd just finished reading a book, to formulate an opinion about it. To me, a recently read novel was like a miniature planet: only a few hours earlier I had been breathing its air and living contentedly among its people—and now I was expected to pronounce a judgment about its worth? What was there to say? *I enjoyed that planet. I believe that planet and its inhabitants are very worthwhile.*

"I liked it," I said. "It was good."

"That's it?" My mother passed me the crackers.

"I thought the story was about claustrophobia," Wallis said. "All the characters are trapped. They're limited by the perspectives they were born with. Even the husband."

"The husband's a total creep," Jill said.

Frowning, Wallis examined a stalk of celery. I was going to have trouble not thinking about her as a little brown cub. "He thinks he's being good to his wife," she growled. "He thinks he loves her. But he can't see beyond the conventions of his time."

The three mothers were nodding. In another hour, I thought, everyone would be gone, and I could be in bed eating an ice cream sandwich.

"It is no use, young man," CeeCee said, tossing her hair. *"You can't open it."*

"I beg your pardon?" her mother asked.

"That's what the wife tells her husband." CeeCee nudged the fan with her foot. "You should try to keep up with the reading next time."

" 'It is no use, young man,' " Wallis echoed.

I stared at CeeCee.

"It's at the very end," she said, leaning back in her chair. "The wife is telling her husband that he can't open her bedroom door because it's locked. Of course there are multiple interpretations. She's saying that he can't understand her—he can't open her mind. And she's obviously talking about sex, too, which they probably aren't having anymore because of her little breakdown. She's closed herself up in her yellow room, or maybe her *womb,* and now she's telling him he can't *come in.* She won't let him knock down her personal entryway and—"

"I think everyone has finished writing down suggestions," Jill's mother said. "Should we see what they are?"

CeeCee stood up. "It must be time for a bathroom break," she said.

Like an old-fashioned butler in a mansion, I said I'd show her the way. Jill stood up as if attached to us by a string, and a minute later the three of us were bumbling into the bathroom, Jill nudging us from behind and then closing the door.

"Okay, what was that about?" Jill asked. "Were you making fun of my mother?"

"I don't think so. I don't think I needed to," CeeCee said. She sat on the counter next to the sink, swinging her pedicured feet back and forth. "This is going well so far, isn't it? Our first meeting? My sister gave me the lowdown on the book; she had to read it in college. I might have read it myself but it sounded slow."

"How inconvenient for you," Jill said. "First you have to be in a book club; then you're expected to read the books."

"I know. It sucks." CeeCee opened the medicine chest and examined the contents of its sticky shelves: a bottle of aspirin, a package of bandages, a wrinkled sponge, some cleanser, a box of stomach meds, a thermometer, a lipstick, a container of baby powder, a toothbrush missing most of its bristles, and a plastic jar full of safety pins.

"What are you looking for?" I asked.

"Just browsing," she said. "What did you and Jill talk about before I got here? Have you told her about your missing dad?"

"He isn't 'missing,'" I said, glancing at Jill. "He's just . . . not around."

CeeCee unscrewed the lid on a plastic jar and peered inside. "Absent, missing, whatever," she said. "If I were you, which I'm obviously not, *I* would be curious. I'd want to know where fifty percent of my cells were from."

39

Jill pulled back the curtain in front of the window, which looked onto the porch. "I wonder if it's too late to switch to regular English."

There was a knock at the door. "Hello? Is this the bathroom?" It was Wallis. She stood on the threshold when Jill opened the door. "They sent me to find you," she said. "Why are you meeting in here?"

"The best book clubs always meet in bathrooms," CeeCee said as Jill and I shuffled aside to make room.

Wallis scratched at a scaly patch of skin on her leg and glanced quickly at each of us. "There were only four books that got more than one vote," she announced. She seemed to be speaking to the towel rack behind me.

CeeCee closed the bathroom door with her foot. "Before we get caught up in business details," she said, "I need to ask you a question, Wallis. Why are you not shaving your armpits?"

Wallis lifted one arm as if to check beneath it. "In most of the world, the women don't shave," she said. The hair under her arms was a thick black tangle, as if twin dark animals had crawled up there to die.

"Is this meeting over yet?" Jill asked.

I told Wallis to hurry up and let us know which books we were going to read.

CeeCee said she was hoping for *The Kama Sutra, The Joy of Sex,* and *Your Difficult Teen.*

Wallis cleared her throat. "The books are *Frankenstein,* by Mary Shelley; *The Left Hand of Darkness,* by Ursula Le Guin; *The House on Mango Street,* by Sandra Cisneros; and *The Awakening,* by Kate Chopin."

Frankenstein was the only one I had heard of. "The mothers must have voted together," I said. "They probably cheated."

Through the open window overlooking the porch, CeeCee and Jill and I heard our mothers starting to laugh. The sound was high-pitched, sharp, and female; it made me wonder whether people consciously changed the way they laughed as they grew up, whether a switch in their heads made them shift from teenage snickering to what my friend Liz called martini laughs.

Jill filled a paper cup with water. "What do you think they're talking about?" she asked.

"Us," I said.

"Definitely," CeeCee agreed. "That's the whole idea behind this book club. They've arranged for us to read the same books they're reading so we can think their thoughts and start living their lives. They want *us* to turn into *them*."

Jill muttered something about conspiracy theories, but I thought CeeCee might have a point. Sometimes I imagined that growing older meant that, at twenty-five or thirty, I'd be forced to weave my own awful cocoon and climb inside it, emerging several years later wearing ill-fitting pants and yammering on about the price of gas and milk. "The Mother-Daughter Book Club and Conspiracy League," I said.

More laughter filtered through the window.

"That's a good idea. We need a title—a name for our book club," CeeCee said.

"Titles are hard." Wallis scratched the rash on her leg.

41

"What about The Literary Enslavement Society of West No Hope?" CeeCee asked.

"Catchy," said Jill.

I suggested The Involuntary Book Bondage Guild.

After exchanging a few more title ideas we went back to the porch, where someone had switched on the overhead light. Outside the screens, fireflies were puncturing the night with their yellow bodies. To them, we might have looked like a collection of oversized creatures in a very large jar.

Wallis picked up the crackers she had brought. We confirmed our next meeting.

"I wish your mother had been able to be here." Jill's mother patted Wallis on the shoulder. "I don't think I've met her. What sort of project is she working on?"

"A book. It's about philosophy. My mother is a philosopher," Wallis said. The lenses of her glasses were covered with specks.

"I thought philosophers were extinct," I said.

Jill asked Wallis if we could read her mother's book.

But Wallis said the book wasn't intended for people like us. We wouldn't be able to understand it. It was only for other philosophy professors to read.

There was an awkward pause.

"Well, this is very exciting!" Jill's mother beamed. "We're like characters in a book ourselves. We were almost strangers to each other a few hours ago, but now here we are, getting ready for something to happen. For the plot to begin!"

"Mom? It's time to go," Jill said.

My mother asked Wallis if she wanted someone to drive her home. Where did she live?

Wallis opened the screen door, letting several moths flutter in. "Weller Road," she growled. "Past the tower."

"Past the old water tower?" CeeCee's mother looked surprised. "I didn't think anyone lived out there."

"We're renting," Wallis said. "I don't need a ride." She pushed through the door and headed into the dusk beneath the trees.

CeeCee raised an eyebrow in my direction. "*There's* a plot waiting to happen. Don't you think so, A?" From that moment on, all summer, she called me A.

Frankenstein

4. PLOT: This word has kind of a bad feeling about it because of terrorist plots and plots to commit murder and plots in graveyards. But in a book it just means the main events in a story and the order they're in.

Frankenstein was slow going at first. It starts with a sea captain writing letters to his sister. He complains about his lousy education and tells his sister he's lonely on his ship and wants a friend. Then, as if by magic, a friend appears: a crazy half-starved castaway who tells the captain that he built a monster. *Now we're getting somewhere*, I thought. I could feel myself sinking into the story. I dug into the box of cereal I was feeding myself by the handful and turned the page.

The phone rang. It was my mother, calling from work. Was I awake yet? she wanted to know.

I reported back in the affirmative. *Every night I was oppressed by a slow fever*, I read, my fingers combing through the crunchy depths of the box. *I became nervous to a most painful degree.*

"Adrienne? Did you hear what I said?" my mother asked. "I won't be home until six-fifteen."

"Okay," I said. "Why don't we ever buy donuts?"

"We had donuts last week. The problem with my getting home later," my mother said, "is that I won't be able to drive you to the pool."

"Huh." I had reentered the book. Victor Frankenstein's family had sent him to college, where he had apparently signed up for Immortality 101: he was spending most of his classroom time watching bodies decay.

"Have any of the girls from the book club called you?" my mother asked. "Adrienne?"

I shunned my fellow creatures as if I had been guilty of a crime.

"Adrienne?"

"What? Don't worry about the pool," I said. "I don't have to get there every day." My mother spent fifty hours a week teaching people about the different uses of *in, at, on,* and *of,* and she was worried about *my* being bored. She must not have realized that I had an impressive to-do list.

Adrienne's list:
1) Read advice columns online.
2) Find out whether a donut-delivery service exists in West New Hope.

3) Train hair to part on the left side.

4) Talk to self in a British accent. *Wot did yew saaay?*

"Put the book down for a second," my mother said. "The problem is that my schedule at work has changed. I won't be able to drive you to the pool at all."

"Oh." I ate a handful of cereal and noticed the trail of crumbs that had followed me—how did these things happen?—across the kitchen floor.

"Which is why I asked if you'd heard from anyone in the book club. I spoke to CeeCee's mother—I think she's going to have CeeCee call you."

Wot did yew saaay? "Why would CeeCee call me?" I asked.

"Because I asked her mother if they could give you a ride to the pool. And it turns out they can, at least Monday to Thursday. They can pick you up after CeeCee's summer school class. I think it ends at twelve-thirty."

I picked up my cell phone and checked for messages: none. "CeeCee doesn't want to hang out with me."

"Well, you don't know that," my mother said. "She's probably as bored as you are. And you need to get to the pool. I'm trying to do you a favor."

"I don't want you setting up playdates for me," I said. Did my mother think I was entirely helpless? "It makes me look pathetic."

"Fine." My mother said she had to get to a meeting. "But answer your phone if it rings. And you saw the note I left on the counter? You'll clean up the kitchen and take out the trash?"

I grew alarmed at the wreck I perceived that I had become.

"What? Yeah," I said. "You don't have to remind me."
But in fact I did forget, and the dirty dishes and the trash
were still in the kitchen when my mother got home.

That night, turning over in bed to prop my knee on a
pillow, I heard something moving through the leaves by the
side of the house. Mr. Finkle, I thought: harassing songbirds
at the feeder. My mother claimed to like cats but detested
Finkle, who staggered away from the feeder several morn-
ings a week with a finch in his teeth, like a heavy man
pushing away from the table after a meal.

I sat up, sweating; when I looked out the window it was
still dark—too early for Finkle, who didn't make his mur-
derous rounds until dawn.

"I know this is it," a voice said. "I was here last week
and scoped it out."

A second, lower voice seemed to disagree.

*I am going to be murdered in my bed because my mother doesn't
believe in air-conditioning,* I thought. My window was open
because fluorocarbons were depleting the ozone. *Being alive
has been nice, Mom,* I thought. *Enjoy your planet!*

"*A!* Are you in there?"

"Who is it?" I asked, peeling the sheet from my legs.

"Come out, come out wherever you are," a voice sang,
just loud enough to thread its way into my room.

"CeeCee?" I crept to the edge of my mattress—the
thick fabric of the night only inches away—opened the
screen, and stuck my head out. CeeCee was standing on

the grass about eight feet below. "What are you doing here?" I asked.

"My mother informs me that I'm supposed to be calling you," she said. "But I don't have your cell."

"Oh. Should I give you the number?"

"Yeah, but I don't need it right now, because I'm already here. Are you coming out?"

"Outdoors?" I asked. In the thicker darkness near the pom-pom blooms of my mother's hydrangeas, I saw the orange tip of a cigarette. "Is somebody with you?"

"Yeah, that's Jeff," CeeCee said.

"Oh," I said. "Who's Jeff?"

"Jeff Pardullo. He's going to catch you."

I looked at the cigarette tip. "I could just come to the front door," I said.

"Look, A. I came all the way over here to see you," CeeCee said. "Just come out the window. That's the plan. Your mom'll hear you if you open the door."

My mother probably wouldn't have heard me. She went to bed at night as if assembling equipment for a difficult voyage, sleeping with a bite plate in her mouth (to keep her from grinding her molars) and a satin eye mask over her face. And she had a machine on her bedside table that played an endless *whssshh*ing of ocean waves against the shore.

"It's not like you're busy. You were only sleeping," CeeCee said. "All you have to do is sit on the windowsill. Jeff does the rest."

How strong is Jeff? I wondered. CeeCee stepped into a narrow patch of moonlight that briefly illuminated her upturned face like a coin. It made no sense to climb through the window. But maybe I didn't want to be bored all summer. And maybe this was the sort of new and invigorating experience my mother had been recommending, one of the ways I could broaden my view of the world.

"All right," I said. "But I have to get dressed. And put on my brace."

"What the hell—is she in a wheelchair?" the Jeff-voice asked.

CeeCee told me to hurry up.

On an unnamed island near the Canadian border, Liz was probably turning over in her sleeping bag, dreaming peacefully under the stars. I put on a pair of pajama pants and flip-flops and a shirt and my brace, and at the last minute—thinking strategically—I picked up my purse so I'd have a key. I could sit on the purse on my way out the window, and I'd have a phone in case CeeCee's plan was to play an amusing joke on me that involved my being kidnapped or killed.

Once I stuck my head through the window again, I saw her out in the yard, fake-boxing with a person who must have been Jeff. I put my purse on the sill and sat on it, perched above them as if on a swing.

Girl Plunges Needlessly Through Window and Mangles Already-Injured Leg, the morning headline would say. I braced my arms against the window frame. "Ready?" I asked.

A pair of hands with knobby fingers grabbed my hips and tugged and lifted me down. I lost a few chunks of skin from the back of one thigh.

"Uooof," a voice said. Whoever Jeff was, I could feel

49

him stagger when I collided with his chest. I grabbed his shoulder to steady myself, and looked up.

He was taller than I was, and his face was interesting but not handsome. His eyes were set deeply and close together, and his eyebrows were thick, like dark slashes of paint. He was probably nineteen or twenty. He smelled like cigarettes and mint, and his cheeks were stubbly, as if he was thinking of growing a beard.

I let go of his shoulder and we started walking away from the house. I had left the window open behind me. I thought about the books I had read in which a character discovers a door into a place she didn't know existed: Alice tumbling down the rabbit hole, Mary Lennox opening the hidden gate to the secret garden, Lucy Pevensie pushing her way through the back of the wardrobe.

"I get so bored at night," CeeCee said. "I have insomnia. Do you?"

"Not usually," I said. "I love to sleep. My astrological sign is the sloth."

CeeCee was twirling a golf club in her hands like a baton. Jeff walked in front of us. "I was lying in bed doing nothing," CeeCee said, "and for some reason I started thinking about our Intolerable Book Bondage Group for Wayward Girls, and I remembered that my mother had told me to call you. What was it about?"

"Getting a ride to the pool," I said.

We had reached the curb. Jeff took a set of keys from his pocket.

"The pool's probably closed," CeeCee said. "But we can drive past it."

I said I was looking for a ride during the *daytime*.

"Well, we need to go somewhere," CeeCee said. "We have a car. I found this old putter in my dad's closet, so maybe we should go to the mini-putt."

Jeff popped the locks on a rusted blue four-door.

"The mini-putt is probably closed also," I said. I had looked at my clock—a parting glance—on my way out the window: it was two-fifteen.

"The best part is that Jeff's decided to let me drive," CeeCee said. "I'm an excellent driver."

Jeff let out a yip—a single high-pitched laugh, like a hyena's. "You're not touching the driver's side of my car."

I paused on the slope of my neighbors' lawn. A chain of events, I thought, was being set into motion, and it seemed very likely that, at some future time, this particular link in the chain would be the one I'd regret.

"What's the matter?" Seeing me hesitate, CeeCee had opened the front passenger door of the car. "A, he's my sister's boyfriend," she said. "Do you think I'd drive off with a total stranger? Do you think I'm an idiot?"

Kind of, I thought. But I got in. She sat in front next to Jeff; I climbed in back.

I wasn't used to driving around West New Hope in the middle of the night, and I didn't like the way the ordinary landmarks seemed to have changed, the trees looming larger, the houses like sinister imitations of themselves.

CeeCee sat sideways in her seat, with her feet in Jeff's lap. "Look at the earring I found," she said. She twirled it in her fingers near Jeff, but he ignored her. "A, are your ears pieced? Jeff doesn't want to pierce his ear."

I had one hole in each earlobe. That was the extent of my fashion sense.

"This would look good on you," CeeCee said.

We drove past the high school and the junior high, Jeff driving with one hand as if barely involved in the car's operation.

"I could pierce your ear for you right now." CeeCee turned around in her seat and faced me. "I'm really good."

I was going to say that I *might* consider her offer, but CeeCee was already worming her way between the bucket seats into the back. "I've got everything we need," she said. "Because I was going to give the earring to Jeff but he doesn't want it. He actually spurned my generosity."

Jeff caught my eyes in the rearview mirror.

"Now he's going to be jealous of you," CeeCee told me, holding the earring—some kind of sparkly stud—near my ear.

We drove past the drugstore and the bakery and then the graveyard, with its gravestones slanting to the left as if in a breeze. CeeCee knelt on the seat beside me, and I let her wipe my ear with hand sanitizer and then sat patiently under the five-watt bulb while she searched for a needle in her purse. It might seem strange that I let her perform this minor surgery. But as we drove past the graveyard I looked at the graves and thought about the bodies underground, all those people lying on their backs doing nothing, and I thought any one of them would jump at the chance to be alive and to be riding in a car with the windows down, the hot breeze of a summer night streaming in. If anyone asked me later why I let CeeCee put a hole in my ear in a moving vehicle, I could truthfully say, *Dead people told me I should.*

But I thought she was going to pierce the lobe, not the flap and gristle of my upper ear.

"Don't yell," she said. She was using a bar of soap as a backstop. "I haven't punched it all the way through yet." She had pushed my head against the window and was leaning over me, her bony elbow on my shoulder, her knee on my leg.

"I think I'm gonna throw up," I said.

Jeff jerked the wheel, CeeCee's head smacked the window, and I felt a slow and painful *pop* as the earring tore a path through my skin. We pulled into a gravel parking lot by the mini-putt. A cloud of dust blossomed like a colorless flower around the car.

I wrenched the door open and leaned out, and CeeCee gave me a tissue for my ear. "Now we'll distract you with some golf," she said. "Jeff can keep score. You'll share my putter."

I stood up and tested my shaky legs, then walked behind her to the wooden shack where Mr. Baxter usually sold tickets. Even in daylight the mini-putt was faded and pale, the sign over our heads reading AIRY GOLF and the artificial turf peeling up at the edges; now, after dark, the battered fiberglass fairy-tale characters lurked in the gloom. "I don't think we'll be able to see the holes," I said.

CeeCee started slashing through the brush beneath the sign. "Jeff, come and help me find a ball."

Jeff sat on the fence, consulting his phone.

"Jeff's moody tonight. We can ignore him. Here." CeeCee found a dented yellow ball. "You first."

My ear was throbbing. Trying not to touch it, I set the ball on the slab of artificial grass that served as a tee. I looked down the length of raggedy carpet toward Snow White, who was dancing with half a dozen dwarves. (The seventh dwarf had been abducted; only his fiberglass foot had been left behind.)

I'd never played mini-golf in the middle of the night and was trying to orient myself. "Aren't you going to be tired during summer school tomorrow?" I asked. The ball collided with the hem of Snow White's dress.

"That doesn't matter. *Je ne me soucie pas*," CeeCee said.

Though I couldn't quite tell where the hole was, I took two more strokes. The ball *thwocked* squarely against the boards.

Jeff climbed off the fence and announced that he had to run an errand. *At two-thirty a.m.?*

"Come back soon," CeeCee called. She tapped the ball into the cup, and we watched Jeff get into his car and drive off.

We took turns at Hansel and Gretel, Jack and the Beanstalk, and the Three Billy Goats Gruff. "That middle goat looks like Jeff," CeeCee said. "Do you have a crush on him yet?"

"Why are we out here?" I asked.

"I needed to get out," CeeCee said. "I can't think during the day, when other people are awake. I feel like everybody clogs up the air with their thoughts."

A pair of headlights painted the weeds in the empty lot across the street. CeeCee crouched behind one of the goats and grabbed the back of my shirt and pulled me down with her; I tumbled over, awkward because of my leg.

"We should have brought something to eat," she said when the car squealed away. She opened my purse and rooted through it. "Do you have any gum in here, or—" She held up my copy of *Frankenstein*. "You brought this with you?"

"I forgot it was in there." I rubbed some gravel off my arm.

CeeCee angled the book so she could read the back cover in a swath of moonlight. "What's a . . . charnel house?" she asked.

"It's one of those aboveground graves," I said. "You know—where instead of burying people underground they build a sort of miniature stone house and put the bodies on shelves inside it."

"Dead people in bunk beds," CeeCee said. "Weird." She lay down on the artificial turf. The wind rattled the birch trees behind us. "Have you ever dug up anything in a graveyard?"

"No." I was afraid to ask her if she had.

She glanced at her phone. "Maybe your father's dead and buried somewhere and your mother hasn't told you. Do you think she's lying to you about him?"

"Why would she lie about him?" I asked.

"I don't know. I don't know your mother." CeeCee gave me the book. "Read me something."

"You want me to read to you? Out loud?"

"Well, I won't be able to hear you if you read to yourself." She tucked my purse under her head, for a pillow. "You don't have to start at the beginning. I'll follow along. Just read something good."

I flipped through the chapters, leaning against the largest of the billy goats and holding the book so its pages caught the light of the moon. *"It was on a dreary night of November,"* I began, *"that I beheld the accomplishment of my toils. With an anxiety that almost amounted to agony, I collected the instruments of life around me, that I might infuse a spark of being into the lifeless thing that lay at my feet."*

"So he's going to flip a switch and electrocute the monster?" CeeCee asked.

"Something like that."

Her face was shaded by the lily pad that belonged to the Frog Prince. "Go ahead. Keep going."

I felt embarrassed, reading aloud in the middle of the night at the mini-putt, but Jeff wasn't back and no one else was around, so I read about the monster coming to life, about his *shrivelled complexion and straight black lips,* and about Frankenstein, his creator, running away and then fainting because of what he had done. I read about the monster tearing around Switzerland, insulted and lonely. My leg started to ache but I ignored it.

"The monster's a good character," CeeCee said. "I like it when he gets ticked off. A total stranger sews him together out of spare parts and then leaves him to wander around and figure out who he should be. No wonder he's pissed."

56

I agreed. I felt a wave of sympathy for the monster, who eventually decided to kill a few people off. Of course he shouldn't have done it, but I understood his reasons. Even though he was huge and strong and ugly, he felt powerless. The world had set him aside. It had no interest in him and nowhere to put him. Every moment of his life he felt he was staring at a giant stop sign, so he finally took hold of it with his oversized corpse's hands and decided to *shake* it.

CeeCee twitched.

"Are you awake?" I asked. Something crawled across my leg but I brushed it away.

She sat up. "I think we should read only monster books," she mumbled. "Vampires, zombies, werewolves. Hunchbacks and lepers." She opened her phone.

"Lepers and hunchbacks aren't monsters." I stretched, feeling stiff. "When is Jeff coming back?"

"Yeah, that's the problem with Jeff. He's not very reliable." CeeCee stood up. "I texted him a couple of times but he won't text back. He probably went to bed and turned his phone off."

I stared at her. "But we can't walk home from here. It's too far."

She shrugged. "Call him yourself. Or is there someone else you want to ask for a ride?"

I pictured my mother tugging off her sleep mask, spitting out her bite plate, and switching off her ocean on her way to the phone. Shoving my book into my purse, I stood up. CeeCee handed me the golf club, which I started using as a cane.

"If you were a character in this book," she said, "which

57

one would you be? I'd have to be the crazy doctor. I'd be robbing graves and sewing flesh together."

"I guess that means I'd be the monster," I said. I was clumsy and large, and here I was, limping down a gravel road at four in the morning, lurching along. Besides, in terms of personality, I seemed to be a little bit of this and a little of that. I was probably some sort of gruesome composite, a hybrid quilted together from other people's moldy castoffs.

I started to worry that I was bending the golf club. A circle of pain had ignited itself within my knee. "Shit," I said.

CeeCee turned around. "What?"

I opened my purse. I had remembered my house key but I'd forgotten that my mother always locked the deadbolts when we were in for the night. And climbing *up* into my bedroom window—without Jeff—would be impossible. I explained this to CeeCee.

"Do you want to stay at my house?" she asked.

"No." That would make things worse. It wasn't that my mother would be mad; she would be . . . confused. And that would make two of us. Dead people had told me that I should let CeeCee pierce my ear, but why had I climbed out my bedroom window? And why was I dragging a golf club around in the dark, with my knee on fire? Inexplicable. "Why didn't Jeff come back for us?" I asked.

"Because he's a jackass," CeeCee said. "He only showed up in the first place because he owes me a favor."

"What kind of favor?" I stopped to rest my leg for a minute.

"I'm going to cut through this way," CeeCee said. "To my house, it's shorter."

"You don't think it's better if we stick together?" I had just spent an hour reading aloud about a patchwork corpse with a special talent for strangling people. From the side of the road, the weeds seemed to reach for us like fingers.

"We can't stick together if we're going to different places," CeeCee said. She told me to keep her father's golf club. "He has plenty of other ones." She walked away, fading into the night like a blot of ink on a piece of dark paper.

When I finally got home, my leg was throbbing and my ear felt like it had expanded to twice its size. I stood, exhausted, on the front lawn, thinking about my mother calling the police to report me missing. But our windows were dark, so she must not have noticed I was gone.

I sat down on the sidewalk in front of the house. It was after four-thirty. I propped my aching leg on a flowerpot, knowing that my mother, as predictable as a metronome, would wake up at six-forty-five, make a pot of strong coffee, and then open the front door to get the morning paper, at which point she would undoubtedly be relieved and amused (ha ha!) to find Adrienne Kathleen, her only daughter—seeker of experience!—her injured leg carefully propped on a terra-cotta pot full of pink geraniums and a battered copy of *Frankenstein* in her hands.

5. CONFLICT: The stuff that goes wrong and ticks the characters off in a book so they get motivated to do things. I guess if nothing went wrong in a book, you'd end up with three hundred pages of somebody watching her grandmother sleep.

*R*elieved and *amused* were not the right words for my mother's reaction. She stepped outside in her yellow bathrobe to get the paper and to nip the dead flowers from her potted plants, and even before she looked up and fully noticed me sprawling across the sidewalk, I knew the more accurate term for what she was feeling was *pissed*.

"Adrienne? What are you doing?"

I waved at her in a gruesome, exhausted attempt to be cheerful. "Hey." I had barely slept, and I was wearing pajama pants, a shirt with blood on its collar, and a dew-dampened Velcro brace on my leg. I had ditched the golf club in the bushes because it was bent and would require the divulging of information. And although I had worked out a speech in my head—a speech full of reason-ableness and calm explanatory phrases—what I ended up saying was, "I went out."

My mother stared at me, a dead geranium leaf in her hand.

She wanted to know who I'd been with, and if I'd been drinking.

"Drinking?" I laughed, making an unfortunate *caw*ing sound. "I was reading a book. *Frankenstein.*" Brushing some dirt and a few crushed insects from my clothes, I pulled myself up. "I climbed out the window. CeeCee came to get me. She has insomnia." Maybe the insomnia wasn't rele-vant. "I don't drink," I said.

"But you climbed out a window in the middle of the night. And there's blood on your neck." My mother's par-tially flattened hair made her head look uneven.

"I pierced my ear," I said. "CeeCee pierced it. But most of the time we were reading." I explained that CeeCee had showed up outside my window to get my cell number, so I climbed out to talk to her. I skipped the part about Jeff and the car and the mini-putt and staggering home in the dark. "So that's it," I said. "End of story. I got locked out."

"Let me look at your ear," my mother said. "And how did CeeCee get here?"

"My ear is fine." I tried to fluff up my hair to cover the injury. "I'll take a shower; then I'll go back to bed."

"You can't go to bed. You have a doctor's appoint-ment at eight-fifteen." My mother glanced down at the sidewalk. Near the place I'd been sitting there was a ciga-rette butt. She nudged it toward me with her foot. "Is that yours?"

"No."

My mother bent down and picked it up. "I'm going to make some coffee," she said. "And I'll read the paper while you take a shower. And after we both have breakfast and get ourselves dressed, I'm going to take you to your ap-pointment. So maybe we should continue this conversation later."

"We don't need to continue it." I tried to sound confi-dent. Dismissive. I limped up the three cement steps to the house. "I wasn't drinking. Or smoking. I was reading a book."

"Go take your shower." My mother unfolded the paper and started to read it.

I looked at her asymmetrical hair and her yellow bath-robe and I knew she wished I were up in Canada with Liz, paddling my way toward physical and spiritual fitness. "You don't need to assume I'm screwing up all the time," I said.

My mother said there was no reason to be so touchy, and we went inside.

My knee was swollen. And sore. Dr. Ramsan frowned and handled my leg as if it were a roast he intended to put in an oven. "It is still bothering you?" he asked, his voice an elegant singsong. Dr. Ramsan wore a turban and had a black beard thick enough for birds to live in. "I'd hoped it would heal a bit faster."

My mother, in a chair in a corner of the examining room, suggested that leaping through a bedroom window in the middle of the night might not have helped.

"You leapt through a window?" Dr. Ramsan looked impressed. "What for?"

"She had some reading to do," my mother said.

I explained to Dr. Ramsan that I'd been out with a girlfriend, and we were reading *Frankenstein* because my mother had coerced us into joining a mother-daughter book club, even though we were too old for such a thing.

"I didn't coerce you," my mother said. "Your teacher is the one who assigned the books. I asked you a few weeks ago about the idea of the book club."

"I wasn't really listening when you asked me, though," I said.

"I remember reading *Frankenstein*!" Dr. Ramsan smiled. "The tormented doctor! I think it inspired me to apply to medical school. Of course, the cadavers we worked with didn't have to be brought to life, so our job was simpler." He positioned my leg so my knee was bent. "Hubris! Does that hurt?"

"No."

"And this?" He pushed at a fleshy spot near the base of my kneecap. I flinched.

"Still tender," he said. "Make another appointment to come back in two weeks. And I advise you to go in and out of houses by walking through doors, no matter the time of day or night. Will you do that?"

"Okay," I said.

My mother went off to make an appointment at the

reception desk, and I asked Dr. Ramsan to check the new piercing—CeeCee's big fake diamond stud—in my ear. He lifted my hair away from my face; I saw him frown. "Literature," he said, turning away to get a piece of gauze. "Books can be very powerful. They bring a feeling of freedom, isn't that right? You almost feel, while you are reading"—he wiped my ear with an ointment that stung—"as if you have entered an alternate life. As if you could be an entirely different person."

I nodded, and he let my hair fall. "Are you doing your exercises?" he asked.

"Yeah. Most of the time. I might go swimming later today."

"Very good. Walk in the water. Swim with your friends. Read for your book club. But no more windows."

"No more windows," I agreed.

An hour later, to save CeeCee's mother the trouble of coming to get me, my mother handed me a beach towel and a bottle of water and my copy of *Frankenstein* and dropped me off at the pool.

It had just opened. I flashed my pass at the gate and, at the shallow end, walked past a dozen little kids lined up in a fleshy, squiggling row for swimming class. I thought about CeeCee showing up at my window. Why did she ask if my mother would lie to me?

I put on some sun lotion and spread out my towel. Dr. Ramsan was right about books, I thought. Books were powerful and appealing because the things that happened in them added up and made sense. In life—at least in my life—a lot of things seemed pointless or random; it was hard to find a pattern in them at all.

I lay down on my towel-covered recliner, propped my open book over my face, and dropped off a cliff into the land of nod.

"Yo. Adrienne. Hey. Are you alive? You haven't moved for two hours."

"What?" I pushed the paperback away from my face. The sky was blinding. I felt like a lower order of species that had recently pulled itself out of the ooze and into the sun.

"Wow." Jill was looming above me. "That's something I haven't seen before. You've got words stuck to your face. I can't quite read them. Hold still a second." She plucked at my forehead.

"Quit," I said. Shreds of Mary Shelley's *Frankenstein*—it was an old and crumbly copy—had cemented themselves to my skin.

Jill sat on the edge of my recliner. "This is not what I was hoping for in a book club. I'd definitely quit if my mom didn't love the mother-daughter idea." She crossed her legs. "Look at you sweating. You've got a jacuzzi full of sweat in your belly button."

"Don't you have to work?" I asked. "I thought you had a job."

"I'm on a ten-minute break," Jill said. "And I don't see why *Frankenstein* is on that reading list. It's not even scary. The monster wanders around wringing his hands and wishing somebody liked him. If he were alive today you know what he'd be? King of the misfits: a school shooter."

I pictured the monster in a soiled black trench coat, holding a gun. He'd done some strangling here and there, but I didn't think he had random mayhem or mass murder in him. "You could have brought me a Popsicle," I said, peeling another word from my chin.

"I don't remember you forking over any money."

A line was already forming at the snack bar, a row of kids shoving each other and vying for position in the shade. But Jill didn't seem to be in a hurry. She started flipping through my copy of the book. "I'm about halfway through this. Are you already working on your essay?" She pointed to a passage that was circled in pen: *It is true we shall be monsters, cut off from all the world; but on that account we shall be more attached to one another.*

"No. That isn't my writing. My mom gave me a used copy."

"*We shall be monsters.* I like that," Jill said. "And it reminds me: there's a rumor going around that you got grounded because you and CeeCee were AWOL last night."

"I'm not grounded. How could I be sitting here if I was grounded?"

"I don't know." Jill put down my book. "That's not a real diamond in your ear, is it?"

"I don't think so." I turned my head toward her. "How does it look?"

She squinted. "Like you're trying to impress someone," she said.

66

I unscrewed the lid on my water bottle. The liquid inside it was hot enough to make tea. "How did you know I was with CeeCee last night?"

"Ha. Believe me: when you work the snack bar, you know almost everything," Jill said. "People waiting in line talk on their cell phones and think I can't hear them. I'm well informed on most subjects. I should be a town crier."

I spilled some hot water onto my chest. "What do you mean?"

"You know: a bard, a griot. Emcee," Jill said. "I'm talking about one of those people in the old days who stood on a corner with a bell and—"

"I know what a town crier is," I said. Why did everyone think English was my second language?

We watched a little girl down the row of chairs making bubbles with a plastic wand.

"Jill, have you ever tried to find your birth parents?" I asked.

She shook her head. "Nope."

"Why not?"

"Why would I? Some woman in China gave me up fifteen years ago because she knew I'd have a better life over here. So that's what I'm doing. I'm having a better life."

"Right," I said. In Jill's list of SAT words, I thought, she could check off *complacent*. "So you don't feel like you're missing something?"

She shrugged. "My parents sent me to Chinese camp for a couple of years so I could learn to say *Hai. Ni hao ma?* But I didn't like the music or the food. And I like my parents. When I was little they used to tell me that out of all the millions of babies in the world, they wanted me. I used to think somebody had lined up a million babies so my parents could look at every single one of them until they decided that I was the best."

"That's cute," I said.

"I know." She took off her flip-flops and walked to the edge of the pool to dunk them in the water. "Wait a minute." She turned around. "Are you asking me about my birth parents because of what CeeCee said about your dad? He's not missing, is he? You just haven't met him. Don't let her start you off on some kind of quest."

"I can't believe you dunked your shoes in the pool," I said. "What kind of quest?"

Jill put her flip-flops back on. "CeeCee's messing with you," she said. "I told you: you and Wallis and I are her punishment. Remember in sociology last year when we were studying 'primitive cultures'? That's what we are to CeeCee. We might as well be cracking rocks and eating snakes in the jungle."

"She's the one who showed up at my house and wanted to go out last night," I said. "It wasn't my idea."

Jill nodded. "Do me a favor. Hold your arms out. Straight out in front of you. Yeah, like that. Now stick your chin forward. There. *We shall be monsters*. Now you look like CeeCee's little creation."

"I'm not her creation." I dropped my arms to my sides. But I remembered limping down the road in the dark while CeeCee rattled on about graveyards and lepers.

Jill checked the clock behind the lifeguard stand. "Two minutes," she said.

More soap bubbles drifted down the row of chairs. I turned to look at the little girl with the plastic wand and saw CeeCee striding gracefully toward us. She popped one of the bubbles with her finger. "What's that on your face?" she asked, looking at me.

"Adrienne's very excited about *Frankenstein*," Jill said. "She's going to tattoo the entire novel all over her body."

"A walking volume," CeeCee said. She licked her finger and scrubbed at my cheek.

"Bodily fluids," Jill said. "It's time to get back to work."

"You're such a good little salesgirl," CeeCee told her. "I need a chair." She spotted an empty recliner near the shuffleboard court and—ignoring the PLEASE DO NOT REARRANGE POOL FURNITURE sign—dragged it shrieking and grinding across the concrete, then wedged it into a narrow slot next to mine. I moved my sandals and my bag to make room for her.

She spread a fluffy white towel on top of her recliner, then peeled off her shirt to reveal a new bikini: metallic gold. Everyone over the age of seven watched. "In half an hour we'll take you into the water for your daily work-out," she said, standing in front of me and uncapping her lotion. "What were you and the SAT princess talking about?"

"Not much," I said. "She thought I was grounded. Because you and I went to the mini-putt."

"No one gets grounded anymore," CeeCee said. "Didn't that punishment go out in the eighties?" She sat down, knees bent, her long legs forming two inverted Vs. "I texted with Jeff this morning. I told him he was rude to you and might have gotten you in trouble. Next time he won't ditch us."

"Oh." I wasn't sure what to say, so I opened my book.

"You know what we should do?" CeeCee asked. "Instead of both of us writing an essay, we should collaborate on a project. You know, like a website. Or maybe a blog."

"The assignment says *essay*," I said. And I knew what "collaborate" meant. CeeCee wanted me to do the work. *Jill just warned me about you*, I thought.

I went off to the bathroom, rinsed my face in the sink, and came back. In the shade of the snack bar, Jill had run out of customers and seemed to be working with a set of flash cards. Her lips were moving.

CeeCee was typing on a mini-laptop.

"What are you doing?" I asked.

"Hang on." Eventually she turned the cute little computer toward me. "Take a look."

The Unbearable Book Club of West New Hope, DE, the screen read. Down the left side was a list of the books we were going to read. Across the top of the page, there were stick-figure icons of four girls, each followed by our names:

Adrienne Haus, President

CeeCee Christiansen, Motivational Speaker

Jill D'Amato, Anal-Retentive Nag

Wallis Gray, X-Factor; Unknown

Under my name was a picture of me CeeCee must have just taken. I was scratching my rump on the way to the locker room, a pallid crescent of flesh in my hand.

"It needs more art, I think," CeeCee said. "And the authors' names, and a couple of links. Then I'll quote what we say about the books during our meetings, and voilà. Summer essay complete." She closed the laptop. "Was it just me, or did Jill's mother drive you bat-shit crazy during that meeting? I want to ram toothpicks under my fingernails whenever she talks."

"You can't count that as an essay," I said, gesturing to the laptop, which CeeCee stowed in her bag.

"Why not?" she asked. "Teachers love PowerPoint and stuff like that. It's a 'creative option.'"

I could already picture CeeCee getting her project back with Ms. Radcliffe's comments: *A+ Very inventive!* "I still think you should read the books," I said.

"Let's be honest, A." CeeCee checked her reflection in a silver mirror. "What is a book about a talking monster going to tell me?"

I hadn't finished *Frankenstein* yet, so I wasn't sure. Closing my eyes, I pictured Helen Keller and Frankenstein's monster and the woman in "The Yellow Wallpaper" standing together on a riverbank, shouting and gesturing in an effort to convey an important message.

"We're going in the water in ten minutes," CeeCee announced.

A ninth grader shouted her name and did a flip off the diving board; she completely ignored him. "Next time we go out, you'll sleep at my house," she said. "Then we won't have to worry about your getting locked out. Or about a curfew."

"You don't have a curfew?" I asked.

"Not really. Not one that anyone remembers."

I put my book down. "I can sleep over," I said. "But let's not drive around in the middle of the night. I'm not sure that's me."

"Maybe it is, and maybe it isn't," CeeCee said. "You should figure that out."

• • • • • • • • • • • •

6. SUBPLOT: This is sort of like the plot's younger brother, the one who tags along behind the big kids who are hogging the toys and having most of the fun. But mostly it means a less important plot.

Would my mother lie to me about my father? I didn't think so. Of course, I sometimes lied or hid things from her—but that was different. The only reason I could imagine her lying to me would be if she was hoping to protect me. For example, maybe she wouldn't want to tell me the truth about my father if he was in prison. I pictured a bearded man showing up at my bedroom window wearing a jumpsuit and handcuffs. Or maybe she would lie to me if it turned out that my father was dying, and he had written to her, trying to find me, because he needed me to donate a kidney or some extra skin or a lung.

"I've been thinking," my mother said as she dropped a laundry basket full of clothes at my feet, "that you might want to come to the office with me and work as an intern."

"Hnn," I said. I was poking around online, imagining my would-be second parent living out of a shopping cart under a bridge. Once he knew where I lived he would want to share custody. I would have to spend my Thanksgivings with him, chewing on turkey bones in a Dumpster.

"Adrienne?" my mother asked.

"What? You hate it when I go to work with you," I said. My mother occasionally brought me to work when I was sick or had a day off from school, and the experience usually didn't end well, because I either broke the paper shredder or copied my face with the copy machine.

"I don't hate it," my mother said. But I could tell she was searching her memory and coming up with something she didn't like. "How about helping me fold these clothes?"

"Okay. In a minute." Without even looking for it, I had just stumbled across a site that offered tips on how to find missing parents. Most of the information was for people like Jill, who had been given up for adoption. But no matter what my situation, the site advised, I should consider hiring an attorney. And I would need a copy of my birth certificate (did it really matter that I was under eighteen?) before I started my search. Or maybe *quest* was the right word.

I propped my foot on the rim of the laundry basket. "Do we keep my birth certificate around here somewhere?"

"Your birth certificate?" My mother bent down to pick up a sock. "I sent off a copy when you signed up for camp," she said. "The original is in the safe deposit box at the bank."

"Why do we keep it at the bank?" I asked.

"Why do you want it?"

"It's just that I don't remember seeing it. I don't know what it looks like."

My mother described it as a piece of paper. "A piece of white paper with writing on it. Time and date. December twenty-first, seven-twenty-six p.m., Sea Haven, New Jersey. It's pretty straightforward."

Why hadn't I ever seen my own birth certificate? Should I be keeping it in my wallet, to prove I existed?

My mother nudged the laundry basket toward me. "You know, folding is something that even an injured person can do, while sitting down."

I stared into the basket. "You put towels in there," I complained. "It doesn't matter whether towels are folded."

"Humor me," my mother said. "They fit in the closet better that way."

I picked through a collection of socks and T-shirts. A disturbing truth: my mother's underwear and mine were the same shape and size.

"Book club is at Jill's tomorrow," my mother said. "Did you finish *Frankenstein* yet?"

"Yeah." Plunging a hand into a tangle of clothes, I remembered a dream I'd had about the book the night before. In the dream I had opened my bedroom closet so I could get dressed, and in the center of the closet (which in the dream was very large, with a chandelier) the monster was rearranging my shoes, ironing my shirts, hanging my jeans on hangers, and mutely offering advice on what I should wear. I felt guilty about him because it seemed to be his job to stand in my closet by himself until I opened the door. His hands were knitted to his arms with thick black stitches, but he was doing his best to keep my wardrobe organized.

"Mary Shelley was a teenager when she wrote it." My mother watched me struggle with a fitted sheet. I could imagine what she was thinking: *My daughter can't even fold laundry. How will she ever write a novel that will be admired for centuries?*

"You don't have to supervise me," I said.

She held up her hands as if to ward me off. "I wasn't supervising. I was asking you about the book. I thought it was sad. I felt bad for Frankenstein *and* for the monster. They seemed like two sides of the same coin."

This had occurred to me also. I knew what the monster felt, at times, trying to be dignified and mature but ending up behaving like a slob and a jerk.

I folded a pillowcase and matched up a couple of pairs of socks; then, when my mother left the room, I went back to the computer. I typed in *lawyers' fees* and learned that most lawyers charged around two hundred dollars per hour. My mother had put my canoeing money back in my savings account at the bank. I could afford about eleven minutes of a lawyer's time.

My mother rumbled into the den, pushing our ancient vacuum. "Are you researching something?" she asked.

"Yeah. Miscellaneous . . . book stuff." I clicked out of the *lawyers' fees* window and looked up *Frankenstein,* then *The Left Hand of Darkness,* which appeared to be about hermaphrodites on another planet. While my mother vacuumed, I looked up *hermaphrodites* and found a link to *Wallis*

Simpson, Duchess of Windsor. These sorts of random connections: what did they mean?

Still surfing around, I stumbled across an anagram finder and typed my name into it: Adrienne Haus. Among the possible anagrams: *Sunnier Ahead.* That was nice. *Use Hind Area.* Not so nice. *Hide Near Anus.* Hm.

The anagram finder didn't come up with much that was interesting for *CeeCee Christiansen* or *Jill D'Amato,* but it turned *Wallis Gray* into *Always Girl, A Swirly Gal,* and *Lily War Gas.* Strange.

The vacuum roared along the carpet in front of my feet. Swinging my legs over the arm of the couch, I typed *Unbearable Book Club* and there it was, CeeCee's "essay" on a new blue background. She must have spent some time updating it. There were a few more photos, including one of Jill—now listed as our book club's Financial Officer—sitting at the snack bar, clutching a wad of dollar bills. I clicked on the stick-figure icon next to my name. Under *personal* I was listed as *widowed;* and under *goals* it said, *I need to dye my hair and get a tattoo.* Wallis's section was *under construction—please check back later.* And under CeeCee's name (she was still identified as our Motivational Speaker) there was a picture of ten perfectly pedicured red toenails in front of the pool.

Jill's house was thick with rugs and curtains, every room wallpapered, as if in homage to the book we'd discussed the week before. There were fuzzy yellow bamboo shoots in the hallway, pink and blue roses in the living room, and, in the kitchen, golden faceless men and women pushing wheelbarrows and carrying sheaves of wheat. "What's that about?" CeeCee asked. She took a picture of the kitchen wallpaper with her phone.

The house was air-conditioned to about sixty-five degrees. Jill's father was partially disabled from multiple sclerosis, and he hated the heat.

Eventually Jill's mother called us to order, and we clustered around two flowered couches in the living room, where the pink and blue upholstery matched the ruffled drapes. There were seven of us again, instead of eight. CeeCee raised her eyebrows in my direction when Wallis told us her mother couldn't come.

As a contribution, Wallis had brought three bananas with her, each dotted with bruises. Jill's mother had set them on a plate. She peeled one and ate it, exclaiming as if it were a marvelous and exotic hors d'oeuvre.

For a while we ate button mushrooms and yogurt-covered pretzels and talked about monster books in general: *The Strange Case of Dr. Jekyll and Mr. Hyde*, *Twilight*, *Interview with the Vampire*, *Dracula*, and *Lives of the Monster Dogs*. CeeCee summarized a few of the slasher films she'd seen, at which point we learned that Wallis didn't own a TV.

"Why not?" Jill asked. She wanted to know if Wallis was Amish.

"Show us your butter churn," CeeCee said.

The collective motherhood in the room seemed to think the lack of a TV qualified Wallis for a Nobel Prize.

"You've probably read more books than the rest of us,"

my mother said. She had apparently forgotten that I was spending my summer reading.

"I read one book a week," Wallis said in her animal's voice. "I made a rule. One book a week, times roughly fifty books per year, over a reading lifetime of sixty years: that's three thousand books." She paused. "I call it the Rule of Three Thousand."

"Three thousand books," my mother said. "But that's so few, for an entire lifetime."

Apparently thrilled with this encouragement, Wallis went on to explain that people who read two books a week, with a few weeks off for travel or sickness, would be abiding by the Rule of Six Thousand.

No one said anything, probably because—mathematically speaking—three of us were humbled and three were annoyed.

CeeCee took out her phone to snap a picture of Wallis, but Wallis immediately turned away.

"I don't want my picture taken," she said.

"Can we talk about the book for a while?" I asked.

Jill tucked her feet under one of the flowered cushions on the couch and started us off. She said she didn't understand why Victor Frankenstein insisted on keeping his creation a secret. "Why didn't he just bring his family together and sit them down and say, 'Hey. Guess what? I made a dead guy, and now he's roaming around killing people'?"

"He was probably ashamed," her mother said. "He must have realized that creating the monster was wrong."

"Maybe," CeeCee said. "But wasn't it worse for him to run away after he brought it to life?" She put her cell phone back in her purse. "He's like a parent who takes one look at his newborn baby and then abandons it."

Jill's mother stared at the two remaining bananas.

"I hope I'm not touching on a difficult subject." CeeCee balanced a plate of stuffed mushrooms on the palm of her hand. "But it does seem relevant, now that I think of it. Right here in this room, we have one person abandoned at birth"—she looked at Jill—"one abandoned *before* birth"—she looked at me—"and one question mark." She looked at Wallis.

"Why am I a question mark?" Wallis asked, without sounding curious.

"Anyway," CeeCee went on, "it's no wonder the monster is screwed up. He has no mother, and his father turns out to be a deadbeat dad. He's a poor nameless orphan."

I had never thought of myself as *abandoned*; the word had a pleasant, dramatic ring to it. "Jill thinks if the monster was alive today he'd be a school shooter," I said, noticing that Jill looked a little snarly.

"That makes sense to me. Neglect breeds violence," CeeCee said. She offered me a mushroom, which gave way in my mouth with a squish and a pop: it had been injected with some kind of cheese.

My mother proposed her theory about Frankenstein and his monster being somewhat the same. Maybe that was the point of most monster books, she said: to point out that everyone had good and evil characteristics, like Jekyll and Hyde.

Finally we talked about the women in the book, who were prone to fainting spells and to getting themselves strangled, and Wallis explained that strangling someone could take up to five full minutes of continuous pressure around the neck. It wasn't as easy to kill a person as most people assumed.

CeeCee said she would remember that information for future use.

The phone rang. Jill's mother excused herself and went off to answer it.

We took advantage of what seemed to be a break in the proceedings. CeeCee's mother and mine talked about yoga, Jill stacked some plates, and I ate another mushroom, wondering whether an evil person lived inside me and was quietly waiting for a chance to emerge.

CeeCee stood up and plucked at my sleeve. "Meeting in the conference room," she said.

I followed her down the hall and into the greenest bathroom I had ever seen: four green walls with green ruffled hand towels and a green furry rug and green-and-white curtains and—on top of the toilet—a crocheted toilet paper–roll cover in the shape of a green hoopskirted doll. I felt as if I'd tumbled into a bottle of kiwi shampoo.

Jill stuck her foot in the door as CeeCee started to close it.

"Why do you want to come in?" CeeCee asked. "You don't like this book club."

"Neither do you," Jill said.

"Good point." CeeCee opened the door and let Jill in. "I think I might be getting used to it, even though it is extremely unbearable," she said. "We should be the *Extremely* Unbearable Book Club—for Irresponsible Girls. I might

81

change our name." She picked up the toilet-paper doll. "What's with the deep-forest theme, by the way?"

"Leave that alone. My mom likes to decorate. And we're not all irresponsible." Jill straightened the crocheted hoopskirt. "Why are we always meeting in bathrooms?"

"I think that's explained in our founding documents," CeeCee said. She opened the medicine cabinet, found a bottle of aspirin, and pried off its lid.

We heard a knock at the door. "That's probably Lily War Gas," I said. "I mean Wallis."

"This group gets weirder by the minute," Jill said. She let Wallis in. Behind the specks on her thick glasses, Wallis's watery eyes glanced quickly at mine. She stepped over the threshold and took in our surroundings as if she were a tourist in a cathedral. "This is beautiful," she growled.

"It's green," said Jill.

CeeCee picked up a bottle of cough syrup and examined the label. "I'm glad we've decided to start making personal comparisons between these books and our lives," she said. "I was afraid our group was going to be too scholarly."

"You aren't even reading the books," Jill said. "And no one else is making comparisons."

CeeCee put the cough syrup away and picked up a can of air freshener—mountain pine. "But don't you want our group to be *relevant*?" she asked. "Isn't that the purpose of a book club? The books don't matter: it's what we find out about each other. We know Jill is an orphan, and we've learned that Adrienne is half an orphan, and—"

"How can I be *half* an orphan?" I asked.

"The point is . . . ," CeeCee said; she shook the air freshener and pointed the can like a weapon at Jill. "Shouldn't we be telling each other our secrets?"

"No. And stop fishing through our stuff," Jill said. "Put that away." She tried to get control of the air freshener but CeeCee was taller and held it over our heads. "I'm the Statue of Liberty," she said. She pressed the button, releasing a long, wet blast in a circle above us. The piney fragrance trickled down on us like rain.

"You are a seriously disturbed individual." Jill finally wrestled the spray can away from her.

Wallis wiped pine scent from the back of her neck. "I thought the idea of the book club was to get ready for AP English," she muttered.

"That's only if you aren't insane," Jill said.

"Where on earth did they go?" It was CeeCee's mother, out in the hall.

In the bathroom, all four of us, as if by previous agreement, went quiet and still. We heard a pair of shoes click-clacking away.

Browsing through the medicine chest again, CeeCee picked up a container of baby powder. "So, twice in a row, Wallis," she said. "Why did your mother decide not to come? I'm starting to think she doesn't exist."

"My mother exists," Wallis said. She turned to me. "I'm like Adrienne. I live with my mother. It's just the two of us. She got divorced."

"Being divorced shouldn't keep her away from the book club," CeeCee said. "Does she think she's better than our mothers?"

"No." Wallis's face was expressionless.

"We obviously have different kinds of moms in the group," CeeCee went on. "A's mom is the teacher/librarian model, and Jill's is the business executive or ruffle queen. My mother's the tennis-playing trophy wife, complete with vibrator in the bedside table. I doubt your mom would feel out of place."

"Your mother has a vibrator?" I asked.

"Everybody over twenty has a vibrator," CeeCee said. "It reduces stress."

Jill took the baby powder away from her. "Sit down over there and stop talking." She pointed to the toilet, then turned to Wallis. "Are we going to meet at your house next week? We'll have to meet your mother eventually, won't we?"

For some reason Wallis looked at me as if I could answer this question for her, or as if there were something about her life that I understood.

"Does your mother even know about the book club?" I asked. "Did you invite her?"

No answer from Wallis.

"Oh. Amazing," CeeCee said. She sat down on the closed lid of the toilet. "You never told her. I'm so impressed! The three of us are showing up every week with our mothers like good little girls, and you waltz over here with your three bananas—"

Jill cut her off. "Wallis, do you want us to meet at your house next time? Yes or no?"

"No," Wallis said. Her hair looked like it had been cut with a kitchen knife.

"Okay. Then we'll meet somewhere else. And I guess we're finished with *Frankenstein* now," Jill said.

There was a knock at the door. "Girls?"

Back in the pink and blue living room, we agreed to move on to Ursula Le Guin's *The Left Hand of Darkness*. My mother had brought a stack of well-thumbed library copies from work. I announced to the group in general that we would be reading about hermaphrodites.

"I don't think that's an accurate description," said my mother, sounding annoyed.

"Hermaphrodites that live on another planet," I amended. "Sometime in the future."

Jill's mother turned to CeeCee's mom. "Dana? Could we meet at your house next week?"

Dana examined an imperfection on her arm—*Is she really a trophy wife?* I wondered—and then said that we could.

My mother hunted around for her car keys and said that she and I would drive Wallis home.

But Wallis was gone. I had seen her leave a few minutes earlier and opened my mouth to tell her to wait, but she threw me a look so cool and bloodless, the words caught in my throat. So I didn't stop her. I watched as she picked up her two uneaten bananas and walked out the side door.

The Left Hand of
Darkness

7. MOOD: The mood of a book is kind of like the mood of a person. It can be funny or sarcastic or wacky or sad. I wonder if the mood of a book depends on the mood the writer was in when she wrote it.

Back in what was quickly becoming our regular spot at the pool, CeeCee was turning the pages of a magazine. "Who has a theory about Wallis?" she asked.

Jill rolled her eyes. "I don't want to start that conversation."

CeeCee held up a picture of a model in a shampoo ad. "You should definitely dye your hair," she said. "It'll perk you up. Jill, don't you think A should dye her hair?"

"*You* don't dye your hair," Jill told her.

"My hair is blond," CeeCee said.

I had just reread the same paragraph for the third or fourth time. It was still hot and I was feeling peevish. My knee was sore, my ear was probably infected, and Jill, who was on a fifteen-minute break from the snack bar, was usurping space at the foot of my chair.

"Maybe red highlights," CeeCee said. "Brown is not an attractive color."

I saw someone walking outside the fence. "Is that Wallis?" I asked. I thought I recognized her archaeologist's shorts. But Jill pointed out that the person I was looking at was a tiny old lady.

"Right: back to Wallis. Here's one possible theory," CeeCee said. "Her mother is dead and divided into a bunch of plastic bags in the freezer. Or, theory number two: her mother is bat-shit insane, and Wallis has locked her in the attic and every night she slides her a tray of food through a slot in the door."

Jill was staring at the side of my head. "Your ear looks like crap, Adrienne." She leaned toward me. "There's a bunch of pink crust growing around the hole."

"Is anyone listening to me?" CeeCee asked.

"You should take that earring out and start over," Jill said. "You have to use fourteen-karat gold or surgical steel."

"Hello? That gold is easily sixteen karat," CeeCee said. "And you probably shouldn't let my mother see that you have it."

I touched my ear. It was swollen. "This earring's your mother's? You said you found it."

"I did. My mother's always losing things. She's very careless." CeeCee adjusted the tiny battery-operated fan on the arm of her chair. "A, admit it. You want to know what Wallis's deal is. You want to figure her out."

Did I? I thought I wanted to figure *myself* out. "She has a rash on her legs," I said.

"That's probably psoriasis." Jill picked up my water bottle and drank from it. "She can get a prescription."

Mr. Vonn, our music teacher, walked by with a newspaper under his arm. His stomach was furry with black and gray hair, and he was wearing a bathing suit printed with musical notes. He wiggled his fingers at us, humming.

"Absolutely no comment," CeeCee said.

I tried to go back to *The Left Hand of Darkness*, but now I was thinking about Wallis.

CeeCee noticed me staring into space. "I bet she's got a little crush on you," she said, turning another page in her magazine. "Didn't I hear her say, 'I'm like Adrienne'?"

"That's only because we live with our mothers," I said. "I didn't skip a grade, and I didn't magically appear in the middle of the school year, and I don't live in the woods."

Jill handed me my empty water bottle. "You make her sound like one of those feral children," she said. "The ones that are raised by packs of wolves."

An image of Wallis as Red Riding Hood filtered into my brain.

Jill picked up my copy of *The Left Hand of Darkness*. A postcard Liz had sent me fell out of the book. *Mosquitoes the size of raccoons here,* she'd written. *No shower for 17 days. All my clothes smell. I'm washing my underwear in the lake.*

"How much of this book have you read?" Jill asked.

I shoved the postcard into my purse. I had finished the first four or five chapters. The main character, Genly Ai, was a sort of ambassador to the planet Winter, where it

was always cold, and where there was no difference between men and women because everybody shifted back
and forth from male to female. Genly had trouble understanding what was happening at first, and so did I.

Jill flipped through the book to chapter seven. "Look,"
she said. "'The Question of Sex.'"

"There's a whole chapter about sex?" CeeCee asked.

"Not the kind you're hoping for," Jill said. "It's mostly
incest. Between two brothers—or maybe a brother and a
pseudosister."

"I don't think it counts as incest if the people are
aliens," I said.

Outside the fence, two guys I recognized from school
were throwing a basketball through a rusted hoop.

"Why are the only people in town this summer either
unattractive or mentally ill?" CeeCee asked.

Jill gave me the book back. What had struck me most
about the novel, so far, was the way the characters were
allowed to change. On the planet Winter, you could be a
certain type of person one day, but then the next day, or
the next week, everyone you knew accepted you as someone else.

"Here's a thought. We could pay her a visit," CeeCee
said.

"You want to visit Wallis?" I asked.

"Why not? You're obviously concerned about her. And
the two of you have a lot in common. Besides, we haven't
seen her in a couple of days. Maybe we could stop by and
check things out."

Like ambassadors, I thought. *Like Genly Ai.*

"Or here's a different idea," Jill said. "We could leave Wallis alone. We could let her *not* shave her armpits. We could let her wear ugly glasses and have psoriasis on her legs."

"They *are* ugly glasses," CeeCee said. "And I notice you used the word *we*. There's so much togetherness in this group. It's really touching."

A cluster of younger boys swaggered past us. I waved to Liz's little brother, Max.

"I hope you aren't flirting with that nine-year-old," CeeCee said.

Jill groaned and got up. "I have to work. Break's over."

A dozen people were milling around, listless, in a scrap of shade by the concession stand. CeeCee and I watched Jill unlock the money box and corral the little kids into a line.

"Our only problem," CeeCee said, filing her nails, "will be getting a car."

Maybe it was the heat, or my knee, or the fact that Liz was away, but I felt irritable and restless. Maybe some sort of change would be a good idea, I thought. Nothing drastic or permanent—just something to make me feel more confident and less like a *blank;* closer to *edgy* and further from *bland.* I spent an hour in the beauty aisle at the drugstore and, remembering CeeCee's suggestion, chose a box of Rich Auburn. It had to be better than my natural shade, which was probably best described as Playground Dust.

In case she might try to talk me out of it, I waited until my mother had gone to a coffee shop with a friend; then I cranked the air-conditioning down to sixty-five, turned the radio to its highest volume, and took the hair dye into the tub. One of my favorite scenes in one of my favorite books is the part in *Little Women* when Jo cuts her hair. Because her family needs money, she sacrifices her "one beauty" and sells her long, thick hair to a man who makes wigs. My hair wasn't long, and my mother didn't need me to sell anything; still, squishing the color around on my scalp, I imagined myself whipping a scarf off my head and astounding everyone with my thoughtfulness and generosity.

I forgot the timer and probably left the dye in too long while I shaved my legs and invented a new kind of cheese sandwich, but I followed the directions otherwise, and then I rinsed and dried my hair and got dressed and reexamined the package, which probably should have been labeled *Firehouse Red*.

"Maybe it fades," I informed the mirror.

The mirror suggested I immediately get into the shower and wash my hair several times. Forty minutes later the color had barely faded, and I noticed that the tips of my ears and an inch of my forehead were the color of blood.

My laptop had been acting a little funky, so I used my mother's ancient computer to look up *how to get dye out of hair*. Solutions involved washing, washing with substances I didn't have, and professional help. Eventually I ended up following a link—*need help?*—which had nothing to do with hair but offered me advice if I had an STD or was pregnant. This site, in turn, led to a page (had my mother been looking at it? was that why it cropped up?) for single parents.

At first I thought it was a dating service, but other than her once-a-month dinners with Carl Schunk, who ran the hardware store, my mother hadn't dated in years. I scrolled through the site. It definitely wasn't about romance. It outlined the risks of being the teenaged child of a single parent.

Apparently, without even knowing it, I had grown up in a scarring environment. Fatherless children, the site warned, were more likely to drop out of school, to be poor, to get addicted to drugs, and to be at risk for identity and gender confusion. I ran a hand through my hair, which was feeling stiff. Kids without fathers, the site said, ended up in jail more often than two-parent kids, and their lives were more likely to end in suicide.

Huh. I hadn't thought about suicide much. And I hadn't done anything—yet—that would land me in jail. *Identity and gender confusion? Really?* I thought of Estraven in *The Left Hand of Darkness* changing from female to male and back again.

By the time my mother came home I had almost forgotten about dyeing my hair. The shocked expression on her face was a quick reminder.

"You're kidding," she said. I could tell that words—entire sentences—were arriving in her mouth, and she was swallowing them back. "How many bath towels did you ruin?" she finally asked.

"What?" I hadn't thought about the towels. The one resting next to me on the floor did seem to be stained.

Maybe she's shocked because I look older and more sophisticated, I thought.

My mother picked up the towel. "I suppose it's not permanent." She tilted her head as if to observe me from a different angle. "Why did you do it?"

To give you money so you can visit Father near his Civil War battlefield. "No reason," I said. "And thanks for the big vote of confidence." I went to my room.

Twenty minutes later my mother knocked on my door. "Do you want to play Scrabble?"

If this was a peace offering, I thought, it was the wrong kind. "You always beat me at Scrabble," I complained.

"I don't *always* beat you." My mother was ridiculously fond of Scrabble. "Adrienne," she said. "I just wasn't prepared to see your hair looking so . . . bright. Come out to the kitchen. I'll set up the board." She lured me out of my room—I put on a thick black headband—by promising to advance me fifty points.

"How's your knee feeling these days?" she asked, once we sat down and picked our wooden letters.

"It's getting better." I flexed my foot.

"I know it's stressful, being injured," my mother said. "You're probably sorting a lot of things out."

I recognized a certain tone in her voice and started to wish I had stayed in my room. "Like what?" I asked. "What am I sorting out?"

"Well, I don't know; maybe you should tell me." My mother set down some letters. "Twenty-six points," she said. "It's your turn."

The intriguing thing about playing Scrabble is that as soon as the board is set up in front of me, I don't know any words. Other than *cat* and *bat* and *rat,* everything disappears from the language drawer in my brain. My mother, on the other hand, who normally speaks English like a regular person, spells things like *qiviut* ("wool of the musk ox") and *hake*.

"Hake?" I asked. "You got twenty-six points for *hake*?"

"It's a type of fish," she said. "You've probably eaten it."

I stared at my letters.

"The reason I'm asking about stress," my mother said, "is that you've got a newly pierced ear that looks infected, and you just dyed your hair, and—to be honest—you've been pretty moody for the past few days. Also, I noticed the website you were looking at on my computer. You left it open. It said something about 'teens in crisis.'"

"Oh. That," I said. "I wasn't really looking at it. It just . . . came up." I thought about the website. Was I at risk? Was my flame-colored hair a cry for help? I managed to get ten points for *beat*.

My mother wrote down my score. "Maybe later this summer, once your leg is healed," she said, "we could go for a trip. We could drive to the Adirondacks or the Poconos."

"We live forty minutes from the Atlantic Ocean," I said. This was a source of tension between us. My mother said she didn't like the ocean, even though she'd grown up at the New Jersey shore. She told me she got a rash from sitting on the sand.

I dipped into the packet of wooden letters and came up with a *J*, an *X*, and a *V*.

"It occurs to me that you've been thinking about your father more often." My mother turned *hake* into *shake* by spelling *quips*. Forty-four points. Why were we playing a

94

game that always proved that she was smarter than I was? "And I noticed CeeCee brought the subject up at book club."

"I can't help it if CeeCee brings it up," I said.

"*Are* you thinking about your father more often?" she asked.

"I don't know. I'm trying to think of a Scrabble word," I said.

My mother filled up the kettle and heated some water for tea. "It was an odd discussion at book club," she said. "But I liked hearing from Wallis about her Rule of Three Thousand. She's an interesting girl. You should try that: try keeping a list of all the books you read."

I felt a prickle of irritation. What was so *interesting* about Wallis? Actually, I had looked up *Rule of 3,000* on the computer, assuming that she had plagiarized the idea from somebody else, but all I had found were a few scattered references to the dangers of climbing more than three thousand feet at a time in the mountains, and some miscellaneous information about a magic card game involving warriors, dragons, labyrinths, beasts, and typhoons.

We each took our turns. Despite the fifty points my mother had advanced me, I was ten points behind.

My phone started buzzing—a text from CeeCee: *What R U doing?*

Not much, I answered. *Hanging out w my mom. You reading L H of Dness?*

Oui. Highly influential. Am planning sex change on ½ of my body.

I turned the word *band* into *husband*.

"Clever," my mother said. "But you might have used the *S* for a plural."

"I don't like making plurals." Why had my mother said I was moody? Just because I was annoyed with her didn't mean I was moody. "Did anybody ever want to marry you?" I asked.

My mother's hand paused on her tray of letters.

"I was just wondering," I said. "Because you raised the subject. Did anybody—you know—ever express any interest?"

"Someone did," she said. "Before you were born. But he wasn't the right person."

"Are we talking about my father?" *And why didn't you ever tell me that?*

"No. This was a different person," she said. "Besides, in my opinion, a *father* or a *parent* is a person who raises a child. I think of your biological father as . . . an anonymous sperm donor."

You made him anonymous, I thought.

CeeCee texted again. *U around later?*

"We used a condom," my mother said. "You're living proof that they aren't a hundred percent effective."

I didn't want to be talking about condoms with my mother. I looked at my letters on their wooden rack: *Yukturx. Krutyux. Tyuxruk.* I used my *X* to spell *ax*, then texted CeeCee: *Can't do tonight. Talking to my M @ the guy she slept w.*

My mother was eighty points ahead.

Ask her how hairy he was, texted CeeCee.

I tried to come up with another word: *Nuktury. Tunkyru.* I seemed to be losing my grasp on my native language.

"I guess the moral of the story," my mother said, "is that sex always involves a risk. And I'm glad that—"

"Why are we talking about this?" I asked, louder than I had intended.

"I thought you brought it up," my mother said. "I don't understand why you're getting so angry. I assumed that you wanted to ask me a question."

This was our bargain, from the very start: *Answer only what Adrienne asks, and nothing more.* I felt like I was playing a game I didn't understand.

It was my mother's turn, but she wasn't looking at her letters. She was looking at me.

2morrow night then, CeeCee texted.

I put the phone down and picked a blank. Of course, I thought: a smooth wooden square with nothing on it.

I bumped the edge of the Scrabble board and jogged the tiles from their places. "You win," I said, tossing the blank back in with the other letters. "I don't want to play this game anymore."

· · · · · · · · · · ·

8. SYMBOLISM: I don't think symbolism comes up very often in real life. It seems mostly to exist in books so that people who like puzzles and hidden meanings can find it.

"That's a weird color," CeeCee said, when I showed up at her house the following night with my fiery hair. "Are you going to redye it?"

"No. My mother hates it, so I'm going to keep it," I said.

"That makes sense." CeeCee nodded.

I caught sight of myself in a mirror. The color made my head look burned, but it seemed to have attached itself to me, as if making a statement: *You are what you say you are, yet you're a joke, a hoax.* That's what someone said to Genly, in *The Left Hand of Darkness*.

I followed CeeCee upstairs. I'd never been in her house, which was four times the size of mine. In her room she had a queen-size canopy bed, an antique dresser and dressing table with a dozen tiny, elegant drawers, and an Oriental rug.

"How did the sex talk go the other day?" she asked. "Did you get any good info?"

"I don't think I want that kind of info," I said, but I told her about the websites I'd consulted about fatherless teens. "I'm a 'person at risk,'" I said, explaining that statistically I was more likely than other people to end up an alcoholic or an addict and to be arrested for a serious crime.

"What kind of crime do you want to commit?" CeeCee started sorting through her underwear drawer.

"I don't know. I don't want to rob a bank," I said. "And I don't want to kill anybody."

"Not yet anyway," CeeCee said. "You probably have to work up to that sort of thing." She threw a tangle of colored fabric into the trash. "I hate old underwear," she said. She nodded at my backpack. "What did you bring with you?"

I showed her: a T-shirt to sleep in, a toothbrush, and *The Left Hand of Darkness*. Was I supposed to bring anything else?

"No, I guess not." CeeCee walked into her closet and emerged a minute later wearing a blue kimono. "I have to take a shower. My hair feels like string." She checked her phone. "You should read to me," she said. "Like you did at the golf course."

"You want me to read to you in the shower?"

"I don't want you to get *into* the shower," she said. "I just want you to read."

99

Like a walking SparkNotes guide, I followed CeeCee into the bathroom, which had two matching sinks, a separate little enclave for the toilet, and a strategically placed marble wall, about four and a half feet high, that divided the rest of the room from the shower. "So I can talk to people and not see their ugly bits," CeeCee said. "I've even talked to my grandma in here; and believe me, under no circumstances do you ever want to see my grandmother naked."

Now and then I had seen my mother naked. Once I had opened the door to her bedroom and seen her walking around wearing only a necklace and a pair of socks. *Are you going out in that?* I had wanted to ask.

CeeCee stepped around the marble divider, hung her kimono on a peg, and turned on the faucet. "God, I love water," she said. "You'll have to read kind of loud."

I leafed through the book, searching for a chapter that would pull her into the plot so she'd read the rest. "You know what *kemmer* is, right?" I asked. "Every twenty-eight days the people on the planet Winter become male or female, depending on who they're attracted to and who they're with."

"Yeah, weird," CeeCee said. "Like getting your period. But I don't get how it happens. Are they all built like Ken dolls most of the time? And then all of a sudden something either sprouts or—"

"The book doesn't go into that kind of detail." I started to read. Estraven had rescued Genly Ai from prison. They hadn't trusted each other before, but now the two of them were thrown together. They were both in danger and had to rely on each other as they tried to escape across the Gobrin Ice.

Fifteen minutes later CeeCee turned off the water and reached for a towel. "You really like this book, don't you? I can tell from the sound of your voice when you're reading."

I did like the book. Though he was middle-aged and black and male, as well as a diplomat and a time traveler, I knew how it felt to be Genly Ai. He was supposed to understand and communicate with the people on the planet to which he'd been sent. But he sometimes felt like he was missing a set of instructions, or a crucial portion of his own brain, and he spent a lot of his time feeling jumbled and alone.

CeeCee put her kimono back on and stepped out from behind the marble wall. "Do you think Genly's gay?"

I flexed my knee. "I don't think that question makes sense on their planet."

She wiped a circle of steam off the mirror. I realized I was watching her and not reading. She turned around.

"What?" I said.

"I'm just wondering. Are you a lesbian?"

"Me?" I laughed—a high-pitched, nervous whinnying sound, like an aging horse with its leg in a trap.

"You don't have a boyfriend," CeeCee said. She was combing her hair.

"But I've . . . been with guys," I said. As recently as February, in fact, I had several after-school kissing encounters with Jason Fenn, who I might have liked better except that he was about eight inches shorter than I was. We met under the bleachers. I had thought about lifting him under the armpits so that his mouth could be closer to mine, but in the end I had just hunkered down and bent my knees.

"What about you?" I asked. "Are you going out with anyone?"

"I don't like the term *going out*," CeeCee said. "Anyway, we're talking about you. We're trying to establish your orientation—whether you're gay or straight." She finished combing her hair, sending drops of water and flecks of conditioner onto the floor. Then she set her comb down by the sink and pressed her mouth against mine.

Iamnotreallydoingthis, I thought. My hands hung at my sides like a pair of dead fish. What did Genly say when Estraven told him he had entered kemmer? *My friend, there's nothing to fear between us.* CeeCee's tongue flickered and crept across my upper lip. Her hair smelled like artificial fruit. "Any reaction?" she asked.

I tried to make a gesture that meant *No comment.* Jason's lips had been crusty and chapped; I'd wanted to bite the little pieces of dead skin from his mouth.

"The problem with guys," CeeCee said, "is they kiss too forcefully. It's like they want to show you their lips have been pumping iron. And they open their mouths too wide. You know what I mean?"

"Right," I agreed. *Am I a lesbian?* I imagined myself wearing a black leather jacket and torn pants with chains, like some of the girls in the gay-straight alliance at school. I picked up *The Left Hand of Darkness;* we walked back down the hall to CeeCee's room.

She put on some music and stepped behind her closet door to get dressed. "Try this on," she said, throwing me an emerald-green scarf. "It'll look good with your hair."

Whenever Liz and I had sleepovers, we spent our time talking, eating junk food, and making fun of shows that we secretly liked on TV. Draping the scarf around my neck and watching CeeCee step out of her closet wearing a short denim skirt and a white tank top, I had a feeling that we were going to do something else.

Her phone let out a beep. She opened it, smiled at the screen, then snapped it shut. "That was Jeff," she said. She retied the green scarf for me and stood back. "He can't find his car keys."

"Was he going to come over tonight?" I asked. He was probably lying about the keys, I thought: he was probably afraid that if he showed up, he would have to heft me through another window.

CeeCee opened one of the tiny wooden drawers in her dressing table and drew a thin arc of brown liner above each eye. "Do you want me to set you up with him?" she asked.

"You mean, with Jeff? I thought he was going out—or in a relationship—with your sister."

"My sister's in Paris, A," she said. "And I have a prediction. Ready? You'll end up making out with Jeff before the end of the summer."

I thought of the stubble on Jeff's chin and the way his face was shaped: like a shovel. "Really?" I asked.

"Absolutely. It's going to happen." CeeCee held out the

eyeliner. "Do you want to use this? You should keep it and use it; I have one I like better." She tossed it into my backpack. "Let's go downstairs."

We left the music on and went down to the kitchen, which was large enough for several chefs to cook in: oversized refrigerator, oversized sink, mile-long stretch of immaculate cabinets, and six-burner stove. "The only thing we use is the microwave," CeeCee said. She got a glass from the cabinet and punched the refrigerator in the stomach, so that it rumbled and then gave her some ice.

"Are your parents asleep?" I asked. I hadn't seen them.

"They might as well be." She started surfing through the cabinets, picking up boxes of cereal, tins of chocolate, bags of rice, baking soda, almonds, pancake batter, and coffee beans. "Why, hello there," she said. From behind two jars of spaghetti sauce she plucked a small bottle of gin. *Beefeater*, it said. The label showed a whiskery man in a red uniform.

"Won't somebody notice that's missing?" I asked.

She tucked the bottle under her arm. "Are you always this nervous?"

We walked through the dining room and down the hall, CeeCee swinging a set of keys on a silver chain. She unbolted the door.

"I don't want to walk a long way," I said.

"We're not going to walk."

We stepped outside and ducked through the puddle of light from the motion detector. The warm air smelled of asphalt, mown grass, and charcoal grills recently extinguished.

"So we're not going to Wallis's, then," I said.

"Of course we are. That's what we've been talking about all week."

"We have?" I asked. "But what about Jill?"

"She wasn't exactly enthusiastic when we mentioned the idea to her," CeeCee said.

We crossed the neighbors' driveway. CeeCee was still swinging the set of keys on their silver chain. When we cut across to the next block, I saw a rusted blue four-door lurking under the trees.

"Is that Jeff's car?" I asked. It was probably near midnight. There were no crickets chirping; there were no cicadas, no barking dogs. "I thought he couldn't find . . ." I looked at CeeCee. "You took his car? How did you do that?" I was trying to piece the evening together, to understand where it might be headed before we arrived.

"Do you want to stand here *talking* about the car, or are you going to get *in* it?" CeeCee asked.

I was a person with horrible red hair and a mound of pink crust surrounding a diamond in her ear. I was at risk, and I had just made out with a girl in a bathroom.

I got into the car.

We slammed the doors and CeeCee unscrewed the cap on the gin, which made a series of ominous clicks as if she were breaking a small animal's neck.

I had taken sips of my mother's beer or wine before, and I had seen my mother drink gin and tonics. But I had never tried plain gin. For which there was probably a fairly good reason. "I'm not very thirsty," I said.

CeeCee held the open bottle toward me. "This," she said, "does not have anything to do with thirst."

A pop-up window in my brain reminded me of three things:

1) the drug and alcohol awareness units we had been subjected to in school;
2) my mother's reaction, if and when she found out—but how would she find out? And look what she'd done, after all, getting pregnant with me by some total stranger;
3) the well-known quotation—but I forgot how it went—about experience being the best teacher.

I put the bottle to my lips and drank.

I had read about people who were alcoholics. I had read *A Million Little Pieces* and *Smashed*, but I didn't remember anyone explaining that gin tasted the way gasoline smelled. I felt it crawl down the back of my throat on a thousand sparkling, poisonous legs. I gasped. CeeCee put the key in the ignition.

"Have you taken driver's ed yet?" I asked. To keep from coughing, I took another sip of the gin.

CeeCee fiddled with something on the dashboard. She turned the windshield wipers and the blinker on and then off. At the bottom of the street, a car chuddered past.

I fastened my seat belt. "How bad was that accident you were in last spring?"

"A, I'm trying to concentrate here." The engine moaned

and then screamed. "Driving is easy," CeeCee said. She licked her lips. "People like to pretend that it's complicated. But it's not much different from bumper cars."

"Except"—I wanted to clarify this point—"that we don't want to bump into anything. Did you turn on the headlights?"

"Whoops: no." We jerked down the street for a few blocks until CeeCee remembered the parking brake. "Now we're smooth sailing. Wave to the family." We drove past my house, which was dark and quiet, and past the bowling alley and through the Towne Centre.

"I thought the plan was to go to Wallis's," I said.

"Yeah. But I can't remember where Weller Road is. I'm not very good at navigating." CeeCee ran her tongue across her teeth while looking at herself in the rearview mirror. "I think we might have gone past it. It's right near that eye doctor's office."

"The eye doctor?" We cruised past a playground and a Gas-n-Go. We weren't in West New Hope anymore.

"You know, the one with the billboard above it. And there's a kind of hill . . ."

"What does the billboard say?" I asked, taking a sip from the bottle. The gin had created a fog in my stomach.

"I don't remember," CeeCee said. "It's an ad. There's a guy's face on it—he looks demented, and he's got his mouth open. And the hill—Hang on a second: it isn't the eye doctor I'm thinking of. It's the dentist."

"Should I look up directions?" I asked. I reached for her phone, which was on the seat between us, but with the car still moving I was getting dizzy. "Maybe we should pull over," I said. "In case one of us has to get glasses or have our teeth pulled."

"What's wrong with your voice?" CeeCee asked. "How much of that gin are you drinking?"

I screwed the cap back onto the bottle.

CeeCee talked to herself for a couple of minutes, then pulled a U-turn, the scenery swinging loosely past my window. The front wheel on my side slammed into a pothole.

"Something doesn't sound very good," I said as a *thuppa thuppa thuppa* noise came from the car.

"It's probably just a flat tire. Look. There it is: Weller Road." CeeCee turned left. "Why do they make places like this so hard to get to?"

Wondering who "they" might be—was this a philosophical question?—I drank some more gin.

Weller Road was a meandering county highway. Most of the streets in West New Hope were tidy and short, and featured ramblers or colonial houses surrounded by artificial wishing wells and fake spotted deer. But the old county highway at the edge of town was overgrown. The houses were scattered, without sidewalks or numbers, and most were set back from the road, among the trees. Turning left onto Weller was like driving from the suburbs onto Easter Island.

CeeCee stopped and took the keys from the ignition, and we left the car, slouched to the right because of its flat tire, at the side of the road.

"Jeff's a little freaked out," CeeCee said. She was texting

while we walked. "I told him he shouldn't have left his keys where I could find them if he didn't want me to borrow his car."

We crossed the narrow asphalt roadway, and I tried to remember why we had come. We were looking for something, or saving someone, or doing something important.

Up ahead, all I could see was a cluster of trees with a path leading toward them. I consulted the red-uniformed beefeater on the bottle of gin in my hand: he seemed to understand our quest and know where we should go.

"Is that the old water tower?" CeeCee asked, pointing at the thicker swath of darkness over the trees.

"Yes. Don't worry; I can find it," I said. Beefeater in hand, I led the way, bushwhacking along past an ancient couch with exposed springs and a crumbling stone skeleton of a building that had long been destroyed. I was Marco Polo and Vasco da Gama and Columbus all rolled into one.

"A, wait. Where are you going?" CeeCee called.

But I forged ahead until we reached it. There it was: the tower, surging up out of the darkness, a fat stone cylinder at least six stories high, with a pointed cap on the top, like a rocket. Or an arrow. Or maybe a finger. I tipped back my head and looked up.

"What are you doing?" CeeCee asked.

I told her to look at the tower carefully. "It's pointing at something."

"It's not pointing at anything," she said.

"What do you think it means?" I asked. I found an old oil drum next to the tower and climbed onto its lid.

"I think it means you drank too much," CeeCee said.

I told her to get me the plastic milk crate I'd just seen in the weeds.

She hesitated but then gave it to me. "What about your leg?"

I stacked the milk crate on top of the oil drum. I looked at my leg. Was that a brace on my knee?

"You're really going to climb that thing?" CeeCee asked.

I apparently was. The evening had acquired its own momentum, the wheels of fate turning, so to speak, and I was reaching for the rusted ladder that seemed to cling, as if barely attached, to the bulging wall. Large flakes of rust were peeling off the metal crossbars onto the palms of my hands.

"Tell me what you see up there." CeeCee laughed.

I held on to the ladder and leaned back. As if by prior arrangement with the universe, a wall of clouds above the tower shifted, revealing a billion silver stars. I was riding toward them on a stone rocket. Soon I would look down at myself on the earth and understand who and what and why I was. "I'm very close to the sky now," I said.

"You're not even ten feet off the ground. But you definitely drank too much," CeeCee said. I heard her rustling in the weeds. "Half the bottle, it looks like. Unless you spilled some of this. Did you?"

My lips were numb. *So this is why people drink,* I thought. *It loosens the ties that hold us to the world.* "My ties are loose," I said.

"Do you mean your shoes?" CeeCee asked. "You aren't wearing them."

I tried to look at my feet, which seemed far below me on the ladder. First one foot and—"Oops." The earth spun slowly, once, and then sped up and hammered itself against me. "Ouch." The pain arrived at different parts of my body one after another—first a poisonous scrape above my wrist, then a cracked bell tolling away in my skull, then the familiar lightning flame in my kneecap. "I have fallen from the sky," I said. And then I threw up.

"Jesus, A." CeeCee was next to me. "Are you all right? Can you move?"

I did a sort of backstroke in the weeds.

"You probably got the wind knocked out of you."

I tried to nod in agreement, but CeeCee's features were revolving on her face like the hands on a clock.

"No sleeping," she said. "Don't go to sleep." A minute later she seemed to be dragging me along the path. "Listen to me, A." My head smacked a rock. "Can you sit up? I need you to focus."

She said something about lousy reception and about Jeff and a tire. "Don't go anywhere." She tucked the gin under her arm. "I'll be right back."

The horizon rocked like a boat. I belched, a small heap of foul-smelling liquid spilling into the grass. I tried to drag myself away from it.

"Hello?" I called. "Is anyone here?" A bead of light flashed on and then off. Several centuries drifted by. Finally I noticed two small creatures coming toward me out of the trees. The larger one turned out to be a woman. She was covered in wallpaper, and she was holding something toward me: it looked like a loaf of bread or a gun.

Politely, I asked her not to kill me.

"How did she get here?" the wallpaper woman asked.

The smaller creature peered into my face. She wore a long white dress: was this Frankenstein's bride?

I tried to explain that CeeCee had kissed me and made me an honorary lesbian, and if they decided not to shoot me, we would all turn back into men before sunrise.

The wallpaper woman put her hand on my forehead. "You didn't tell her to come here?"

The murdered bride shook her head.

"I'll get a blanket." Someone used a cloth to wipe my hands and face.

Another decade crawled by. The dark sky with its unreliable stars was revolving around us.

"You shouldn't have come here," said the murdered bride, kneeling beside me. "It isn't safe."

A set of headlights appeared on the horizon.

I waved to them as if flagging down a ship.

"I see her; she's over there," a voice said; and as if they were only products of someone else's imagination, the wallpaper woman and the murdered bride turned back into fictional characters and disappeared.

9. DIALOGUE: Conversation between characters. Which makes me wonder why conversation between three characters isn't called trialogue. Which would lead to quadralogue and pentalogue. Quotation marks are usually used.

—Shit. You left her like this? When did she pass out?

—I don't know. Twenty minutes ago. *A, wake up.* She didn't have this towel around her when I left her.

—What do you want to do with her? Disgusting: there's puke all over the place. I just stepped in it.

—A, can you hear me? It's CeeCee. You have to wake up.

—Where did she get this towel if you didn't give it to her?

—I don't know. There's all kinds of crap out here; she must have found it. We have to get her into your car.

—The car you stole from me?

—The word is *borrowed.*

—The car you drove into a ditch?

113

—A pothole, Jeff. And that's what a spare tire's for. You got a ride here fast enough, so it's not a big deal. Come on. Take her feet.

—Man, she's deadweight. Is this the same girl from the mini-putt? She looks different. She looks . . .

—Be careful of her knee. She has a bad knee. You can't drag her like that!

—Make her stand up, then. What's she saying?

—"I don't speak Voidish." It's from a book.

—She's a real intellectual, huh? She better not puke up my car.

—Jeff, stop! Stop it! Just take her feet. I'll get the door.

—Why don't we drop her somewhere and make her parents come and get her?

—Because she only has one parent—and that parent isn't going to see her like this, or find out.

10. POINT OF VIEW: In this essay, I am using the first person, because it's my point of view. If Dr. Ramsan had written this instead, he'd probably use the third person ("she" or "Adrienne"). He would also get a higher grade on this project, because he's older and has to be smart if he went to medical school.

"A water tower?" Dr. Ramsan asked. We both stared at my knee, inflated to twice its normal size. "You were actually climbing it? A rusted ladder? In the middle of the night?"

My mother was pretending to read in the waiting room. She had driven over to CeeCee's first thing in the morning, having consulted her kitchen calendar and discovered that I had an appointment with Dr. Ramsan (he had clinic on Saturdays) at nine a.m. I had woken up on CeeCee's Oriental rug to the sound of my mother's voice repeatedly demanding, "Are you *drunk*? Adrienne?"

Dr. Ramsan bent and straightened my leg several times. "May I ask—" He paused. He was so polite.

"It's not a very big tower," I said, with one hand on my skull; I was trying to keep my brain from exploding. "And the ladder doesn't go all the way up anymore. I was climbing it because . . ." I tried to remember what my reason had been. Something to do with symbolism? "I guess I wanted to see . . . the view."

"A view at night. Of what?" He pushed on either side of my knee with his thumbs.

"Ow. We were trying to find somebody's house. It's a person we know. We wanted to find out where she lives, but—" I remembered the wallpaper woman and the murdered bride and—had I seen a gun? "I need to lie down." I felt twirly and nauseated and, though I had just showered, I could still smell the stench of the clothes I had slept in. My mouth was a saliva-filled marsh, boggy with pockets of vomit and gin.

Dr. Ramsan moved a pillow to the head of the paper-covered table. "And if you had found the person you were looking for and located her house? Then what?"

"Um, I'm not sure. But I think—" Trying to remember what had happened once we reached the tower was like pulling fish from a muddy pond: flashes of memory kept darting and slipping beneath the murk. "I think I did see the person we were looking for. But how did she know we were there? It was confusing."

"As I suppose climbing a tower in the dark most often would be. You should have a tetanus booster because of this scrape." Dr. Ramsan circled my wrist with his thumb and fingers and examined my forearm. "I notice your mother hasn't come in with you this time."

"She's kind of sick of me lately," I said. I had staggered behind her out of CeeCee's bedroom, steering myself down the stairs by the handrail, a ribbon of vomit snaking its way up my throat. My head was pounding and my knee was on fire. My mother had looked for CeeCee's parents (someone from their cleaning service had let her in), but they were apparently out playing golf. "So much for 'I don't drink,'" my mother had said when we got in the car.

"Being a parent is difficult," Dr. Ramsan said. I saw him notice my hair. "And people your age are often attracted to danger. It's a—what do you call it?—an elixir."

He wiped something that stung into the cut on my arm; I closed my eyes. But as soon as I closed them, I felt dizzy and saw the dreamlike figures from the night before. I had definitely seen Wallis; she was the little dead bride in the nightgown, and she had warned me that I wasn't "safe." (Safe from what?) But had I seen her mother? And was she really holding a gun? "Can alcohol cause hallucinations?" I asked.

Dr. Ramsan took a coil of gauze from a package. "Typically, hallucinations occur with withdrawal rather than occasional use. How much, and how often, are you drinking?"

"It was only last night," I said. "My mother probably won't believe me anymore, but I don't drink."

I sat up, and Dr. Ramsan bandaged my arm. If he had

kids of his own, I thought, they were probably mild-mannered boy and girl geniuses, happily doing calculus and physics in the second grade. "What sort of hallucination did you have?" he asked. "Do you mind my asking?"

"I don't mind." I liked Dr. Ramsan. "Two people," I said. The inside of my head seemed to be coated in an oily fog. "They came out of the trees. And they were either dressed up, or they were wearing costumes—or maybe nightgowns. At first I thought they were characters out of a book."

"Go on," he said, as if he heard this sort of thing often.

"One of the people was definitely real," I said, concentrating on Dr. Ramsan's perfect black beard, like a garden of hair on his chin. "But the other one seemed more . . . fictional. And when my friend came to get me and bring me home"—I remembered Jeff's hands gripping my legs—"they disappeared." I felt for a lump on the side of my head. Maybe I was insane. "Do you think the entire thing was a nightmare?"

"I don't think you dreamed you were climbing a tower," Dr. Ramsan said. "So part of your evening must have been real." He shined a penlight into my eyes and then noticed my ear. "This doesn't look good."

"Yeah, sorry about that," I said, as if my ear—not to mention my knee—were something I had borrowed and was supposed to be taking care of.

He cleaned the piercing and told me to soak my ear twice a day in salt water.

"By the way, I'm not usually attracted to danger," I said. "Up until now I've led a pretty boring life."

"Boredom is good!" Dr. Ramsan looked pleased. "Boredom is why God invented books. Are you still in your book club?"

"Yeah. We're reading *The Left Hand of Darkness*," I said. "By Ursula Le Guin. I don't usually read sci-fi, but I like it."

"I will look for it at the library," Dr. Ramsan said. "In the meantime: ice for your leg, after any activity and at least twice a day. The pool is fine: but no towers, no climbing through windows, no mountaineering, no high-wire acts, no parasailing, no bungee jumping. Am I leaving anything out?"

"Probably not," I said. "Thanks."

"You're very welcome. Take good care."

We shook hands. I went to find my mother in the waiting room.

On the way home in the car, I rolled down my window, sucked up a lungful of hot, damp air, and said, "I already apologized twice. Maybe you didn't hear me."

"I did hear your apology," my mother said. "Now I'm hoping for an explanation."

"I don't think I have one of those," I said. The only explanations I could come up with sounded odd or substandard:

1) I was trying to live up to my potential as a troubled child in a one-parent home;
2) I had been pressured by a whiskered man in a bright red uniform;
3) I was being a jerk.

"People *die* from alcohol poisoning, Adrienne," my mother said.

"I know that." We were driving along the world's curviest road: I felt like I was strapped into a roller coaster. "I don't drink," I said. "If I knew how to drink, I wouldn't have had that much, would I?"

We stopped at a light. My mother turned the vents in my direction; they exhaled a puff of warm air on my legs. Near the side of the road, an old woman was sitting in a plastic wading pool with a dog, rinsing herself and the wagging, furry animal with a garden hose. "Then what's this about?" my mother asked. "Was it just a whim? A failed experiment? Was it CeeCee's idea?"

That's a good strategy, I thought. *Let's blame someone else.*

The woman was soaping up her dog; I wondered if she was using shampoo or—

"Adrienne?" my mother asked.

"It wasn't CeeCee's fault," I said.

The light turned green. "I wasn't suggesting it was her *fault,*" my mother said. "Still, maybe CeeCee isn't someone you should be spending a lot of time with."

I pointed out the *irony* of that statement, given that my mother, along with CeeCee's, had created the Unbearable Literary Society for Impossible Girls.

"The what?"

"It's just a nickname," I said.

My mother turned left onto Powell, the street where we lived. She wanted to know if CeeCee and I had gone to a party. She wanted to know if we'd been seeing boys.

I paused. "No." Technically, I hadn't *seen* Jeff (I'd had

my eyes closed), even though he had dragged me into his car. And if he was over eighteen, he didn't count as a boy. I decided it was preferable not to explain that CeeCee and I had been driving around in a borrowed car without a license.

We pulled into the driveway.

"I hope this doesn't have anything to do with our conversation the other night, when we were playing Scrabble," my mother said. "You're only fifteen, Adrienne. That's very young. I was twenty-eight years old when—"

"I know how old you were," I said. "And I haven't had sex, or anything close." I remembered CeeCee leaning toward me in the bathroom, the fruit-and-syrup smell of her hair. "I don't have a boyfriend and I'm not a lesbian, so you can stop worrying about me; I'm probably . . . frigid."

My mother frowned at the steering wheel. "I'm not sure why you're saying that," she said slowly. "Do you—"

"Mom, please. Do we always have to talk about sex? That's all we talk about anymore." I unbuckled my seat belt, but my mother grabbed my wrist and kept me in the car.

"I want to understand what's going on with you," she said.

I pulled away; I felt like a book she was trying to open.

"I mean it, Adrienne. What are you doing? Who are you turning into?" She was shouting now.

"Don't ask me that!" I shouted back. Then I threw up again, barely managing, before I did so, to open the door.

Maybe because she felt bad for yelling at me when I was clearly in a weakened condition, my mother made a bed for me on the couch. She brought me a can of ginger ale, a pair of aspirin, and a plateful of crackers.

"Thanks," I said.

"You're welcome." She stuck a straw in the ginger ale. "I need to run some errands," she said. "And then I'm getting my hair cut. I guess you could spend the day reading. Did you finish *The Left Hand of Darkness?*"

"Almost," I said.

She brought me a grocery bag, in case I had to be sick. "You're done with sleepovers for the rest of the summer."

"Okay," I agreed. It seemed we were talking about how to punish somebody else—some foolish, risk-taking person we were both exasperated with and yet fond of. *I sure hope the kid straightens herself out.*

My mother handed me the TV controls. "What was that name you used for the book club?"

I repeated it for her. "We made up a bunch of names," I said.

She nodded, then took a sip of my ginger ale. "It's hard for me to get my mind around the idea that a book club could be a bad influence on a person," she said. "I don't want to believe that it can. I remember when you were ten or eleven, I read you *To Kill a Mockingbird*, and for a year you wanted to be a lawyer like Atticus Finch."

I bit the edge off a cracker. "I was ten, Mom," I said. "I barely knew what a lawyer was."

"Of course you knew. You were very bright."

I noticed she had used the past tense: I *was* bright. She probably thought my IQ was diminishing.

I remembered the guy in *Flowers for Algernon,* getting

gradually stupid. "I don't think it's fair for all my role models to be taken from books," I said. "How am I supposed to stack up against Atticus Finch or Anne Frank? I don't know any Nazis. Why don't you just compare me to Aslan?"

"I don't think I've been comparing you to anyone," my mother said. "Where did that come from?"

"Nowhere," I said. "Or from the backseat of my brain."

The phone rang, and my mother went to the kitchen to answer it. When she came back, she said, "Some people see Aslan as a stand-in for Jesus, by the way."

"Perfect." I bit into a cracker. "I just saw him as a really important lion."

"I guess it's all in how you look at him," my mother said. Then she picked up her car keys and left me alone.

I spent an hour or so sleeping and channel surfing and licking the salt from an assortment of crackers. I texted CeeCee: *You get in trouble for last night?*

Non, she texted back.

I told her I was flat on my back with a case of the whirlies. *Come over?* I asked.

It took her a while to answer. *Busy,* she finally said.

My thumbs hovered, indecisive, over the keypad. Was CeeCee mad about something? I wanted to ask her if she'd seen Wallis. I wanted to ask her if Jeff had carried me—preferably in his arms and not over his shoulder—up to her room.

Feeling antsy, I got off the couch and tried soaking my ear. Then I tried on the eyeliner CeeCee had given me, but it made my eyes—maybe because they were bloodshot—

look as if they'd been surgically implanted in my face. Just looking at myself in the mirror, I vacillated between thinking that my funky new look had potential and understanding that I was stuck in a no-fly zone between ridiculous and bizarre.

It was time to get out of my own head and into someone else's. I found my mother's copy of *The Left Hand of Darkness* and went out to the front lawn with an oversized beach towel and a bag of ice for my leg. I spread out the towel and lay down. "Hi, Genly," I said when I opened the book. Soon Genly was explaining both to me and to Estraven, his hermaphrodite frenemy, what it was like to be a permanent member of a particular sex. Turning the pages, the ice bag leaking all over my leg, I tried to imagine the people I knew shifting back and forth: my mother periodically growing a beard and impressive pectorals, and our neighbor, Mr. Burgess, stopping by to complain about his PMS.

A shadow darkened the page; I turned around.

Jill was behind me, straddling her bike. "Wow. Something happened to your face," she said.

"I dyed my hair," I told her. "And put on some makeup."

She climbed off her bike and let it drop to the ground.

Inside the novel, marked by my finger, Genly Ai and Estraven were poised at the edge of the Gobrin ice field. I imagined them tapping their feet and consulting their watches, waiting for the moment when I would open the book and allow them to get back to the business of being alive.

"Did you get grounded this time?" Jill asked.

"Why do you always think I'm grounded?" *Was* I grounded?

"Welcome to the information age. Word gets around." She sat down in the grass. "You didn't call me, I noticed. You put on your makeup and trotted off to Wallis's without me."

"CeeCee thought you wouldn't want to come."

Jill spun the wheel of her bike. "Are you going to tell me what happened?"

"I'm not sure yet," I said.

Across the street, two little girls were prancing through the spray of a sprinkler.

"How come you're not at work?" I asked.

"I was. But then somebody pooped in the pool," Jill said. "They're closed for cleaning. My sincere advice to you? Don't ever put your mouth near that water." She straightened her businesslike black ponytail. "I figure if I sit here long enough you'll probably tell me what happened," she said. "Because you probably want to tell someone. And I'm the only person available." She combed her fingers through the lawn. "You have a lot of quack grass in your yard," she said.

I tried to go back to *The Left Hand of Darkness,* but I couldn't read with Jill waiting next to me. "All right." I put down the book. "CeeCee invited me to spend the night. I didn't know we'd be going to Wallis's. But somehow she took Jeff's car—she must have taken the keys from him earlier—and we drove around and opened a bottle of gin. We were drinking—or I guess *I* was drinking—and we got a flat, because it turns out CeeCee's a lousy driver."

"What a shock," Jill said.

"And we weren't sure where Wallis's house was," I went on, feeling as if I were explaining the evening to myself as much as to Jill, "so we ended up in the dark at the water tower." I paused, because the rest of the story was unclear. "And for some reason I climbed the tower, partway, and then I fell. And I got sick because of the gin."

"We're talking about puking," Jill said. She spun her bicycle wheel again. "So after all that, you never made it to Wallis's?"

"We didn't have her address," I said. "And you know Weller Road. The houses are all stuffed back into the woods. They look almost abandoned—like railroad cars. But we were definitely near Wallis's."

"How do you know?"

The little girls across the street were squirting each other with water guns.

I hesitated. "Well, I'm not positive," I said, "but I'm pretty sure that I saw two people. One was Wallis, so the other one had to be her mother." I was trying to work through the fog in my head. "They were wearing long dresses that were probably nightgowns."

Jill blinked. "Did you talk to them?"

"Not really."

"So they were just standing around in their night-gowns," Jill said. "What was Wallis's mother like?"

"I'm not sure," I said. "It was dark. But I woke up at one point and it seemed like she was taking care of me. You know what it was like? It was like that scene in *A*

Wrinkle in Time where those nameless creatures find Meg and they touch her with their tentacles and end up bringing her back to life."

Jill nodded slowly. "Wallis's mother touched you with her tentacles."

"I didn't say she had tentacles."

"Okay." Jill asked me what CeeCee's reaction to "Aunt Beast" and Wallis had been.

"I don't think she saw them," I said. "She went to meet Jeff so he could change the tire. And when she got back, Wallis and her mother had disappeared. I guess they went—"

"Poof: back to their railroad car," Jill said. "And left you choking on your vomit out in the woods."

I hadn't thought about that. But they had probably known that Jeff and CeeCee would be driving me home. I decided not to mention the possibility that Wallis's mother had been holding a gun. "Forget the railroad car," I said. "Forget the whole thing." I moved the melted ice off my leg. "How did you even know I was out with CeeCee last night? How do you always seem to know what I've been doing?"

Jill pulled up a dandelion puff. "Duncan got a phone call last night. He lives next to Jeff, and Jeff needed a ride somewhere because two girls absconded with his car."

Duncan—a grade ahead of us—had gone out with Jill for a few months; they were still friends. "Duncan texted me about it this morning," Jill said. "He told me to make sure I was never alone with Jeff. He calls Jeff 'the eel.'"

"He doesn't seem that bad," I said, remembering that CeeCee had predicted I would kiss him.

"Jeff does what CeeCee tells him to do." Jill stood up. "Who knows what the two of them have going on?"

The little girls across the street had gone indoors. I told Jill what my mother had said about the Unbearable Book Club: that we were the only group she had ever heard of who could experience book club membership as a negative influence.

"I think she's right," Jill said. "By the way, do you have anything to eat? Maybe a hamburger? That's part of the reason I stopped by. I'm really hungry."

I hadn't eaten anything but crackers all day and my stomach felt like an empty cavern. "What do you want? Frozen waffles? Noodles?"

"No, I'm craving meat," Jill said.

"Meat?" I grabbed her arm so she could help pull me up. "You're a vegetarian."

"That's only at home," Jill said. "I took a stance, so, you know, I feel like I should stick with it. But I really like meat, so I eat it as often as I can at other people's houses." She chained her bike to the metal railing by the front steps and we went inside. In the kitchen, she turned the radio to a country station and opened the freezer. "Aha: this looks promising." She held up a package of frozen sausage, then rummaged through the cabinets for a frying pan. On the radio, a singer howled out his love for a cheatin' wife.

"I hope your mom knows that not everyone in the book club is a criminal," Jill said. "I mean, look at me: I have an actual job, and I don't steal cars or trespass in the middle of the night or have a drug or a drinking problem."

"CeeCee doesn't have a drinking problem," I said. "She didn't drink. I'm the one who got drunk."

"Go ahead. Defend her," Jill said. "Just don't fool yourself into thinking that, outside this book club, you're going to be friends." She dumped the entire package of links into the frying pan. "I sincerely hope you have maple syrup to go along with this sausage."

I gave her the syrup.

Jill wielded a metal spatula against the spattering links.

"Do you still want to be a nurse?" I asked. There was something disturbing about the idea of waking up in a hospital bed with Jill's face being the first thing you'd see.

Jill said she did.

The voice on the radio clawed its way through an octave.

"But how can you already be sure of that?" I asked. "I mean, you could join a motorcycle gang or hitchhike to Alaska. We don't have to graduate high school and head straight to college."

"Don't be ridiculous," Jill said. "We *are* the people who go on to college. That's what we've been raised for."

"You make us sound like farm animals," I said.

Jill nudged the links around in their cauldron of fat.

I got two plates from the cupboard. "You made sixteen sausages," I said, staring into the pan.

"Yeah, I like sausage." She created a bed of paper towels on one of the plates. "Anyway, I'm going to graduate and go to college and become a nurse. Because that's what I've always wanted to do. Pretty soon we can drain these little piggies."

Twenty minutes later we were dipping the last of the sausage into a greasy plateful of maple syrup.

"Man, I feel sick again," I said. "My mother told me I should stick to white bread and crackers. Now the house reeks of pork." I put our dishes in the sink. "Sorry we didn't call you last night." I walked Jill to the door. "I don't think CeeCee's as bad as you say she is. But you're right about Wallis. If she wants us to leave her alone, we should leave her alone."

Jill unlocked her bike from the railing. "It's probably too late for that," she said.

11. FORESHADOWING: This is one of those words teachers write on the board and draw a line through. Fore/shadowing. A shadow/before. It means a hint or a clue, and it usually doesn't point to anything good.

"*T*he most important thing," Jill said, quoting from *The Left Hand of Darkness*, "*the heaviest single factor in one's life, is whether one's born male or female.* I'm not sure I agree with that. What about being born poor? Or being born with one arm?"

"Or being born with an *extra* arm," CeeCee said. "One that sticks out of the middle of your forehead."

We were gathered in CeeCee's living room for round three of the Society of Feminine and Literary Despair. The meeting hadn't started, and still I had a bad feeling. My mother had made a beeline for CeeCee's mother as soon as we arrived, and she didn't look happy; then there was the paper grocery bag Wallis was carrying tucked under her arm. Wallis and CeeCee and Jill and I were circling the buffet table, trolling for food; but even with a plate and a fork in her hand, Wallis didn't put the grocery bag down. I remembered Jill's word from our first meeting: *ominous.*

"What do you think they're talking about over there?" Jill asked. She gestured toward the mothers, three of whom (Wallis's mother hadn't come—she was busy, or she didn't exist, or both) were huddled in a corner near the grand piano. We couldn't hear what they were saying—the living room was huge, with a cathedral ceiling, a fireplace big enough to cook a human being in, and a U-shaped leather couch that probably seated a dozen people—but given the recent tension between my mother and me ever since "The Episode of Adrienne and the Booze," I had a good idea about their topic of conversation.

Mom #1 (mine): I didn't raise Adrienne to turn out to be such a lush. She was supposed to be normal. And smart. It turns out she's an idiot.

Mom #2 (Jill's): We chose our daughter from a lineup of millions, making sure we picked one who wasn't a derelict.

Mom #3 (CeeCee's): I certainly hope that Adrienne, who has no more personality than a fruit fly, isn't going to try to blame my daughter for her absurd behavior.

"Maybe they're discussing the book," Wallis said.

My mother was gesturing, slicing the air with the blade of her hand. About an hour before we left for book club, she had found the bent golf club in the bushes. "Why do I think you might know something about this?" she'd asked.

"Or," Jill suggested, "maybe they're talking about Adrienne's evening with Aunt Beast."

CeeCee pursed her lips and nodded; Jill had taken it upon herself, about ten minutes before my mother and I rang the doorbell, to fill CeeCee in.

I stared across the table at Wallis, who was filling her plate with deviled crab. I'd definitely seen her that night. But here she was, as if nothing had happened—except for that creepy paper bag clamped under her arm.

CeeCee added a radish and a hunk of cheese to the edge of my plate. "They might be setting up guidelines for tonight's discussion," she said. "No graphic references to transsexualism. No drawing diagrams of what might have happened between Genly and what's-his-name, out on the ice."

"I don't think they consummated their friendship," Wallis said, her mouth full of food. "Their union was strictly metaphorical."

CeeCee widened her eyes and mouthed these words back to me: *strict-ly met-a-phor-i-cal.*

"Just think if one of us turned into a guy every other month." Jill pointed at me with a plastic toothpick shaped like a sword. "You'd get a big old patch of hair on your chest. You'd start hitting on girls."

"I'm sure Adrienne would be a perfect gentleman," CeeCee said.

Wallis refilled her plate. "This food is very good."

Jill inserted a bacon-wrapped slice of melon into her cheek. "Did you guys know that there are animals in the . . . whatever, the animal kingdom, where the male has the babies? I think it's starfish. My mother and I were talking about it at breakfast."

"A frank discussion of sex at breakfast is very healthy," CeeCee said.

"Actually, it might have been the sea horse," Jill said. "I think it was."

"I have a statistic," CeeCee said. "Did you know ten percent of Americans are gay? That means that, here in this room, one of us has to be a lesbian. I already asked Adrienne—in fact, we took her out for a test run—but she says she's not."

"What kind of test run?" Jill reached for a chocolate.

"It wasn't a test run," I said. I knew that CeeCee kissing another girl would be seen as stylish, erotic. My kissing another girl would mean harassment for at least a year. "Anyway, ten percent of us would be less than one person. That's point-seven people."

"Or point-three-five of two different people," Wallis said.

"*Your* mom is single." Jill poked my arm with her plastic sword. "Maybe that explains the missing dad. Short hair. No sign of a male-female romance—"

"Are you telling me my mother is a lesbian?"

"Are you girls discussing the book without us?" Jill's mother asked.

"No worries, Mom. Take your time." Jill waved with her sword, and the mothers began chatting again, in their corner of the room.

The front door opened, then closed with an expensive

134

and satisfying thud, and CeeCee's father paused in the doorway, briefcase in hand. He was handsome and tall, like an ad for vigorous, silver-haired older men. He seemed to pose for us; he waved and smiled, showing his teeth. "Hello, ladies."

"Hello, the Dad," CeeCee said. "He's home from work so he can work at home. There's no end to working for a living, is there, Dad?"

"Apparently not," her father said. "Have a good discussion."

Jill's mother abandoned the adults-only corner and picked up a plate, oohing and aahing over the food. She said she couldn't remember the last time she'd done so much reading. She wasn't sure she would ever be a member of our Three Hundred Club: was that the name we'd come up with?

CeeCee made a gun with her thumb and finger and shot herself in the heart.

"Those have meat on them, Jilly," Jill's mother said as Jill speared another globe of bacon-wrapped melon. Then she turned to my mother and CeeCee's: "We're ready to start over here."

Wallis tucked the paper bag between her feet when she sat down.

Discussion didn't go very well at first. We talked about politics on the planet Winter, and about whether it was sexist to say that women are more sensitive than men.

Jill's mother said something about male and female sea horses, which we all ignored. Then someone brought up the subject of men getting pregnant and having children, which led us to a discussion of Mr. Crandall, the geometry teacher, who everyone at school assumed was gay. It turned out that Mr. Crandall and his male partner had hired a surrogate. "They rented a womb," Jill's mother said, "and they're having twins."

CeeCee's mother was leaning forward: I thought she was trying to look past me, but then I realized she was staring at my ear.

I untucked my hair.

Jill said Mr. Crandall was her favorite teacher, but she never imagined any of the teachers at West New Hope high school having flesh-and-blood families or kids; she thought of them as an alien species, spawned in the utility room by the furnace. She imagined them sleeping under the wooden desks in their rooms.

"Like vampires," I said.

CeeCee yawned. It was too bad, she said, that, since he appeared to have his own impressive pair of man-boobs, Mr. Crandall couldn't give birth and nurse a baby himself.

"Leave poor Kevin Crandall alone," my mother said. "He's allowed the unmitigated joys of family and children, isn't he?"

All three mothers started to laugh. They laughed a bit longer than seemed appropriate.

"I think somebody spiked the punch," CeeCee said.

My mother stopped laughing.

"Whoops. Bad joke. Is it time for a break?" CeeCee picked up the empty juice pitcher and left the room.

I looked at Wallis. Maybe she had her mother's gun in that bag, I thought. I wondered how much it hurt, to be

136

shot. I wondered if I could use the tray of melon balls as a shield.

Jill stepped on my foot. "Are you coming?" she asked. She and Wallis and I found CeeCee in the kitchen, at the black granite island in front of the sink.

"I thought it was written in our constitution that we have to meet in bathrooms," Jill said.

"Ordinarily that's true. But I know the bathrooms in this house already," CeeCee said. "There's nothing in them but toilet paper and soap."

"There's nothing but toilet paper and soap in our bathrooms, either," Jill said.

Wallis held the paper bag in her hand.

CeeCee opened a packet of lemonade and dumped it into the pitcher, sending little nano-whiffs of sour powder into my nose. "Well?" she asked. She was looking at me.

"Well, what?"

She added water to the pitcher and stirred. "We have two meetings left. Are we going to talk about it, or not?"

Wallis set the bag next to the sink. It was halfway between us. If she made a sudden move I could try to slap it to the floor.

CeeCee sighed. "So, Wallis," she said. "You might have noticed that Adrienne and I showed up at your house a few nights ago."

Wallis looked unconcerned.

"Jill thinks we were just being nosey, and I admit I've been curious; but I think all three of us suspect that something's not right over there on Weller Road."

"Everything's fine," Wallis said.

137

CeeCee kept stirring. "You've been pretty secretive, to be honest. And you didn't invite your mother into the book club."

"She's really busy," Wallis said. Her voice was thick, as if she had swallowed a mouthful of syrup.

"Anyway," CeeCee went on, "we made a little field trip last week. An investigation. Unfortunately, we ended up with a sort of emergency—"

"Adrienne tripped," Jill said, "and a bottle of gin spilled straight into her mouth."

"But even with the confusion caused by the alcohol," CeeCee said, "Adrienne seems to think she saw you that night. She says she saw both you and your mother, but when Jeff and I showed up you ran away."

"I don't know what Adrienne saw," Wallis said.

I'm not sure whether other people have this ability, but even with my eyes wide open I can picture something—a memory—letting it run like a DVD in my head. So even while I was watching CeeCee stir the pitcher of lemonade in the sink, I could see the two white-gowned figures coming out of the woods. "Get Wallis to open the bag," I said.

CeeCee stopped stirring.

Wallis's mother had definitely been holding something. "It looked like a loaf of bread," I said. "I saw it. And Wallis brought it here in that bag."

"What looked like a loaf of bread?" said Jill.

I turned to Wallis. "Was it a gun? Did your mother have a gun in her hand?" I asked.

We all looked at the grocery bag on the counter.

"What kind of gun looks like bread?" muttered Jill.

"Girls? Knock-knock?" Jill's mother was standing in the doorway. "I hate to interrupt, but we wanted to talk about next week's meeting. And we were also hoping . . . Wallis, sweetheart, would you mind coming out here for a minute?"

My mother and CeeCee's were hovering like birds of prey in the hall.

"Wallis, honey?"

"You can talk to her in front of us," CeeCee said. The grocery bag waited on the counter. "She doesn't mind."

Jill's mother approached slowly. "We just thought it might be nice for one of us moms to drive Wallis home. And meet Wallis's mom."

"My mother's not home right now," Wallis said.

"When will she be back?"

"She's out of town." Wallis pushed her glasses up on her nose. "I can take care of myself," she said.

Silence dropped over the group of us like a cloth. My mother asked if there was a way to reach Wallis's mother.

Wallis said she wasn't sure, but her mother trusted her to be on her own.

"Sweetheart," Jill's mother said. "You're fifteen."

"Fourteen," I corrected. I remembered lying on my back in a puddle of vomit while the stars bumped and zig-zagged overhead; I knew the wallpaper woman had stood above me, peering down as if at a baby in its crib.

"You can't stay home alone," my mother told Wallis. "I think you should stay with one of us. Would you need to pick anything up at your house?"

"No," Wallis said. She glanced at me, then unrolled the

139

top of the grocery bag, which turned out to contain a hairbrush, a bar of soap, some underwear and socks, and a copy of *The House on Mango Street*.

"You *packed*?" I asked.

"I'm glad those socks didn't shoot anyone," Jill muttered.

My mother put her hand on Wallis's shoulder. "You'll come home with us, then?"

Wallis tucked the bag under her arm. "I guess I could do that," she said.

The House on Mango Street

12. RHETORICAL QUESTION: Rhetorical questions are almost always used by adults who want to make other people feel bad. For example, a teacher might ask, "Did you think it was a good idea to show up in class without a pencil?" These are questions you can get in trouble for answering.

"Weren't you just telling me I couldn't have any more sleepovers this summer?" I asked. My mother and I were having a not-very-subtle but whispered conversation in the hall outside CeeCee's kitchen.

"You think this counts as a sleepover?" asked my mother.

"Why wouldn't it count?" I asked. "If she sleeps at our house isn't that *sleeping over*?"

Someone pushed through the swinging door to the

kitchen and I caught sight of Wallis standing at the granite island as if marooned.

"I'm not going to argue about the definition of *sleepover*," my mother said. "She'll stay for a night or two. What's the problem with that?"

Wallis gives me the creeps, I wanted to say. "Why can't she stay with Jill or CeeCee? Their houses are bigger."

"Because you and I offered. That's why."

CeeCee's mother walked past us and the kitchen door swung open again, revealing Wallis standing in the very same place, looking steadily and unperturbedly at me. "Is there something going on here?" my mother asked. "A problem between the two of you?"

A problem? I said there wasn't.

"All right. Then I'll drop you both off at home and go pick up some groceries. You know where the air mattress is, I hope?"

Yes, I knew where the air mattress was; didn't I live at our house?

"Wallis? We're ready to go," my mother said.

"Thanks so much for coming to book club. It was lovely to see you," CeeCee said, opening the door for us when we left. She made a phone with her thumb and finger. "A— call me," she said as Wallis and my mother and I walked to the car.

At the top of the hall closet, I found the air mattress and some sheets and a blanket and an extra pillow; in the bathroom drawer I scrounged up an unused toothbrush (Wallis hadn't packed one) in its crinkly box. I would have put the blow-up bed in the den, but my mother had just bought a new set of bookshelves, and, surrounded by a dozen boxes of books, they were in pieces all over the floor. I stared down at the mess and briefly considered inflating the mattress in my mother's room, but decided I would rather not deal with the parental anger when she got back.

I lugged the plastic-smelling mattress out of its package and unfurled it on the rug in my room. "This might have a leak in it," I said, attaching the pump and inflating the bed while Wallis watched. Putting sheets on the mattress was awkward—like dressing a shark. "Maybe I was wrong about the gun," I said. "And maybe you're mad at me for spying on you. You probably think I'm an imbecile. But I know I saw you that night."

"I don't think you're an imbecile." Wallis's expression didn't change.

"You were wearing a white nightgown," I reminded her.

"I don't wear nightgowns," Wallis said. "Can I borrow a T-shirt to sleep in?"

I gave her my Delaware Blue Hens shirt. She put it on in the bathroom; it came down to her knees.

"Is your mother really away?" I asked. "Or is there . . ."

"What?"

"Nothing," I said, and together we contemplated the blow-up bed, already softening in the middle. Insects were making their electric noises in the trees.

I went off to the bathroom, brushed my teeth and changed into my pj's, and came back to find Wallis already tucked beneath the covers. She had taken off her glasses, and her eyes were small and dark and round, the eyes of an animal peering out of its burrow. "Why did you call me Lily War Gas?" she asked.

I explained about the anagram finder.

"Oh." She stared at the ceiling while I brushed my hair. "Actually, Gray isn't my real last name."

I stopped brushing. "What's your real last name?"

"Well, now it's Gray," she said. "But I used to have a different name. My mother changed it."

"Do you mean, when your parents got divorced?" I stepped over her mattress and climbed into bed.

We heard my mother come in with the groceries. She quickly whapped them away in the cupboards, then stuck her head through my bedroom doorway and presumably counted us: *one, two.* "Wallis, do you need anything?" she asked. "Should I turn out the light?"

"*I* don't need anything; thanks," I said.

Wallis said she might read for a while. "But I don't want to disturb Adrienne."

My mother left the room and came back with a head-lamp on an elastic band—the one we had bought for my camping trip. She gave the headlamp to Wallis, who had put her copy of *The House on Mango Street* by her bed. "See you in the morning."

"Your mother's nice," Wallis said. She put the band around her knobby head and turned it on. The circular beam wobbled across the ceiling and came to rest on the wall right in front of me. "It's too big."

That's because it isn't yours, I thought. "You have to adjust it." I cantilevered the top half of my body over the edge of the bed and tightened the strap. I could smell the soil-like

144

smell of Wallis's hair. "Try it now." Just before I pushed myself back to my pillow, I noticed a scar that began above Wallis's ear and jutted into her hairline. It made me feel shivery. "What's that from?"

She touched the shining, uneven patch of skin. "It's just a mark."

When I tried to get a better look at the scar, she switched on the headlamp. She looked like a cyclops, and when she turned toward me she nearly blinded me with her bluish-white beam.

The next morning I woke up to the sound of voices in the kitchen. When I shuffled down the hall in my pj's and flip-flops, conversation stopped.

"Why aren't you at work?" I asked my mother. I could smell French toast but the griddle was cold. Eggshells and bread crusts littered the sink.

"Because it's only seven-fifteen. You got up early for a change. I hope we didn't wake you. Wallis and I have already had breakfast."

I noticed that Wallis was wearing my mother's yellow bathrobe. "Am I interrupting or something?" I had never borrowed my mother's robe. I stared at the eggshells in the sink.

"We were just talking about books," my mother said. "I was telling Wallis that my favorite Jane Austen novel is probably *Northanger Abbey*. It's a novel about reading. About a girl who has her head in the clouds and bumbles along thinking that life is a book."

Well, lah-dee-dah. "She sounds like a real weirdo," I said.

I took an egg from its plastic egg-shaped home in the refrigerator door and turned on the griddle. In the bread department, we were down to two ancient whole-wheat heels. I checked for mold, then quickly submerged the heels in a cinnamon-and-eggy mixture.

"*Northanger Abbey* always reminds me of Adrienne," my mother told Wallis, who blinked appreciatively behind her thick lenses. "That kind of dreaminess, I mean. But I haven't been able to convince her to read it."

"That's because you've already summarized it about a hundred times," I said.

My mother asked me whether I'd gotten up on the wrong side of the bed—probably a rhetorical question, so I didn't answer.

The first piece of French toast stuck like glue. I'd forgotten the butter. "Shit." I used a spatula to scrape up the blackened, soggy bread and catapult the doughy mess into the sink. It landed with a wet *whomp*ing noise, like a squid being hurled against a rock.

"Adrienne," my mother said.

"Sorry." I turned off the stove.

"Do you and Wallis have a plan for the day?" my mother asked.

Did she mean separately (I hoped) or together? "I'm going to the pool." I dumped a cylinder of shredded wheat into a bowl, then crushed it flat with the back of a spoon. "Are we out of milk?" I stared into the refrigerator. "You just went to the store."

"I didn't realize we were running low on milk," my mother said. She was doing the crossword. "And we only had a quart left." The empty container was next to the sink, where Wallis was pushing eggshells down the drain.

"What am I supposed to eat?" I asked.

"You could make a fried egg," Wallis suggested.

"Adrienne doesn't like fried eggs, for some unknown reason," my mother said.

"The reason I don't like fried eggs," I explained, "is because they're disgusting."

"You have such high standards," my mother said. She suggested that I stay home from the pool for the day and get some things done around the house.

"What things?" I had already put sugar on my shredded wheat; now I stared at the haylike mixture, considered my options, and decided to eat it dry.

"Do you remember offering to reshelve the books?"

I groaned. *Offering* wasn't the right word: as punishment for my recent lack of good judgment, aka my drinking episode with CeeCee (and my mother still didn't know we'd been driving around in a car that belonged to someone nicknamed "the eel"), I had agreed to alphabetize and reorder our collection of books. This had struck me as a pleasant, mindless task when my mother brought the shelves home from the store; later, counting up the mysteries my mother hoarded under her bed, the boxes of "sale books" she had hauled up from the basement, and the twelve-foot span of volumes on the floor-to-ceiling shelves in the cattle chute, I estimated that we owned a gazillion books.

"I don't want to do that today," I said.

"Why not?" My mother stood up and cleared the

147

dishes, moving around me because I was eating standing up. "Maybe Wallis would help you."

I said that I usually worked better alone.

Wallis wandered off to get dressed.

"Are you all right? You seem pretty crabby," my mother said.

Chewing the biscuit without milk made me feel like a horse. Miniature javelins of straw protruded from between my teeth. "How long is she going to stay?" I asked.

"Until her mother gets back," my mother said. We heard my bedroom door shut with a click. "Or until she has somewhere else to go."

Should it have bothered me, that day and the next, that Wallis wore my headlamp strapped to her forehead even in daylight? That she tucked her mattress under my bed and followed me around the house like a shadow? That she took long baths and began to smell like my mother's shampoo?

"Do you mind my being here?" she asked. This was the second day of her visit, and we were trying to assemble my mother's bookshelves in the den. We had managed to put them together with some of the wrong (unfinished) sides facing out, and then had to dismantle them. Then I lost the pegs that were supposed to hold the shelves together.

"I guess you're used to being alone," Wallis said when I didn't answer. (I was trying to look distracted by my search for the pegs.) "I like being alone, too. Do you talk to yourself?"

"Why would I talk to myself?" Backing up on the rug away from the shelves, I accidentally knelt on the hammer. Tears flooded my eyes.

"That looked like it hurt," Wallis said. "Was that your bad knee?"

I breathed through clenched teeth.

"Do you want me to look at it?" she asked.

"No, thanks," I said.

She picked up the hammer and seemed to weigh it in her hand. "I think of my life as a book sometimes, the way you do."

"That's mostly my mother's theory," I said. "Do you and your mother get along?"

"Yes," Wallis said. "We're very close."

"Even though you don't know where she is, and she didn't tell you when she's getting back?"

Wallis's expression was smooth, almost blank. "She left me a message at home yesterday. She'll be back soon."

I stacked some of the shelf pieces behind me. "You went home yesterday?"

"I walked past the pool and saw Jill," she said. "We talked through the fence."

Perfect, I thought. I was stuck at home because of Wallis, while she was strolling around town being social. "Are you going to walk home today, too?" I asked. "In case your mother left another message?"

She probably heard the snarky but hopeful tone in my voice. "Maybe," she said.

I told her she should feel free. And—though she had

found the pegs and helpfully lined them up on the couch—I repeated that I would rather work on the bookshelves alone.

Being rude to Wallis was tiring somehow—I've always found guilt to be exhausting—so I shut myself in my room and ate a handful of semisweet chocolate before doing my physical therapy and getting dressed. Wallis was gone by the time I had finished. *Good.* I texted CeeCee, who hadn't been answering her phone, and then I closed the front and back doors and turned the AC on. Let Wallis ring the bell, I thought, when she wanted to come in.

I checked my phone. Still nothing from CeeCee, but there was a text from my mother, just sent from work: *Have you got the shelves fixed yet?*

No, I hadn't fixed them. What was I, a carpenter?

We can set them up when I get home. Maybe you and Wallis could finish alphabetizing today.

Sigh. I had already collected the *A*'s (of course my mother owned a dozen Austens), intending to move them to the top left shelf in the hall, stashing the *B*'s and *C*'s immediately below. But when I cleared off the books that were already taking up space on those shelves, I discovered a colony of flesh-colored spiders and their cottony eggs. I ended up spilling twenty or thirty volumes onto the floor.

I texted my mother: *You don't need me to alphab within each letter, do you?*

She texted back: *Order them the way a librarian would.*

Resisting the impulse to shovel the books into the yard and then set them on fire, I poured myself a glass of mint

150

iced tea, sat down in front of my mother's desktop, and did a couple of Sudoku online. I looked at a video about a sloth crossing a road in Australia. Finally I created a new blank document for my mother: *Books*. Beneath the heading I typed the letter *A*. I went back to the hallway and shuffled through the paper- and hardbacks. *Alvarez, Abbott, Achebe, Atwood, Atwood, Anderson, Andersen, Amis, Adichie, Allende, Allen, Agee, Austen, Austen, Austen, Austen, Austen . . .* I picked up *Northanger Abbey* and read the first sentence. *No one who had ever seen Catherine Morland in her infancy, would have supposed her born to be an heroine.* This was the novel—apparently a portrait of low expectations—that reminded my mother of me?

I put Catherine Morland in a stack with the other Austens and randomly opened a few other books. Opening a book in the middle of a chapter always made me feel like I was interrupting a group of strangers, wandering unannounced into their villages and apartments and taxis and slums.

Could I be an unlikely heroine?

I imagined the Librarian of Congress insisting on sitting down to interview me. We would probably sit across from each other at the kitchen table. I pictured him as an old-fashioned man, something like the white-haired smiling Quaker on the oatmeal box, with a piece of parchment and a feather pen. I imagined him revising his earlier classification:

Haus, Adrienne. 1. Unlikely heroines—Nonfiction.
2. Drunkards. 3. Inhospitable book club members.
4. Sloths.

My phone was vibrating on the table, doing a buzzing circle dance.

"How's it going with the new roommate?" Jill asked.

"She isn't here right now," I said. "But I'm stuck at home. My mother has turned me into a slave-librarian." I could hear splashing. "Why is Wallis staying with me instead of you?" I asked. "Maybe tomorrow she should stay at your house."

"Nope. Not going to happen," Jill said. "For some unknown reason, she seems to like you. I have a theory about this. Do you want to hear it?"

"Not really," I said.

"I'll tell you anyway. Whatever her situation is at home, even without all those guns being baked into loaves of bread, Wallis doesn't like it. Maybe she's lonely, or maybe her mom's antisocial. So she's decided to experiment. She's developed a crush on your mom—that's pretty obvious— and she's trying her out. It's a little fantasy. You know: *What would it be like if I lived in an ordinary house and had a normal family and didn't live in a railroad car by a crumbling tower?*"

"I never said she lived in a railroad car." Jill was probably picturing Wallis as one of the kids in *The Boxcar Children*, catching fish in a stream and sweeping the pine planks of her home with a handmade broom. "I don't think she has a *crush* on my mom," I said. "But my mom definitely likes her. Probably because she's polite. And neat. And smart. And not me."

"Hey, maybe your mom will decide to adopt her," Jill said. A whistle blew in the background. "Then you could write your summer essay about what it's like to have a sibling all of a sudden."

I tried not to imagine my mother coming home with a set of bunk beds, or presenting Wallis and me with matching lunch boxes on the first day of school. "Wallis is too old to be adopted."

"Oh no, she isn't," Jill said. "Haven't you seen those sad little pictures of 'waiting children' on local TV? People give older kids up for adoption all the time. I think there's a law that lets you drop them off in Nebraska."

"Maybe I can buy her a one-way ticket there," I said. I heard the clank of the cash box—the sound of Jill being useful and earning money.

"Have you started the new book?" she asked.

"No. We just finished the last one," I said. I missed Genly Ai.

"I read the first twenty pages," Jill said. "It's short but you have to go slow. I can't tell if these little sections are paragraphs or chapters. And I don't know who this person is talking to—this Esmeralda or Esperanza: is she talking to me?"

"*I'm* trying to talk to you," I said. "What if Wallis doesn't want to leave? I don't want her living here forever."

"Well, you can't kill her off. Not in real life," Jill said. "Unbelievable: we're out of fudge pops."

"Tragic," I said. "So am I going to like this book?"

"Not sure," Jill said. "At first I felt like I was reading a little kid's book, but I think there's a creep factor coming. Somebody's going to end up dead or abused."

"Great." I looked down at the pile of books on the floor and thought about Wallis's Rule of Three Thousand. "Do people really drop their kids off in Nebraska?"

"Yeah. I guess they have extra room out there," Jill said; then she hung up the phone.

After talking to Jill I had a brainstorm: I realized I could alphabetize the books on my mother's computer. I finished typing in the authors whose last names started with *A* and hit "sort." *Ding!* I was a genius. I rewarded myself with a dish of strawberry ice cream (Jill's mention of fudge pops had made me hungry) and used a dish towel to get rid of the spiders so I could shelve through the *C*'s. Sitting back down at the computer, I noticed that my mother had left her email open. This was obviously not an invitation to read her email; still, without giving it much thought one way or the other, I clicked on her in-box.

She had gotten a bunch of boring messages from people at work (*Please note meeting time change*) and several pleas from a Nigerian lawyer representing our long-lost millionaire relatives killed in a plane crash.

Farther down in the queue was a message from my aunt Beatrice, my mother's sister. My finger dangled above the mouse; then, as if making up its own little fingery mind (my mother didn't have any secrets, did she?), it punched down.

There was a long string of emails going back and forth, so I scrolled to the bottom. My aunt was going to Thailand in September and my mother was jealous. My mother told my aunt about the book club. My aunt asked about me.

She's doing okay, I think, my mother answered. *It's a diffi-cult age.*

Difficult how? my aunt asked.

My mother said she had caught me drinking. She said I'd dyed my hair. *Not terribly flattering,* she wrote.

I felt my face heat up. Did I email people in order to comment on my mother's appearance?

A few lines later, she told my aunt that I'd been asking about my father. *And she's been out all night once or twice. She denies it but I suspect there are boys involved.*

So my mother assumed I was a liar.

What does she want to know about her father? my aunt asked.

I'm not sure. And it's hard to know what to tell her.

How about trying the truth? I thought.

I know what you're saying. You don't want her repeating your big-gest mistakes, my aunt wrote.

"You did a lot of work here," said a voice behind me.

I almost leapt out of my skin. *Wallis.* "Where did you come from? I locked the doors." I logged out of the email account, then realized (I didn't have my mother's pass-word) that I wouldn't be able to get back in.

"I wasn't outside. I was in the basement," Wallis said.

"What were you doing in the basement?" My mother thought I was "difficult." The cursor blinked mindlessly on the screen. "Are you wearing my shorts, Wallis?" I asked.

"Yes." Wallis looked down as if to double-check. "Your mother said I could go through the bags near the washer and dryer."

"Oh." The shorts—and now I also recognized the

155

T-shirt—had probably been rescued from a collection of clothes I'd outgrown.

"You're up to *D*," Wallis said. She started moving books around on the shelves. From the back, wearing my shorts, she looked like a smaller, neater version of me. "Have you read *The House of the Scorpion*?" she asked.

I said I hadn't.

"It's about clones." Wallis knelt on the floor and started sifting through the *E*'s and *F*'s on the rug. "Your mother has a lot of good books. Have you read *Rebecca*?"

My aunt said my mother had made a mistake. "No."

"Have you read *Brave New World*?" Wallis asked.

The mistake was my mother getting pregnant, I thought.

"Or how about—"

"No," I said.

The mistake they were talking about—the big irreversible error of my mother's life—was me.

13. HYPERBOLE: For a while I thought this was pronounced "HY-per-boll," which made me picture a giant bug—the hyper boll (weevil). But actually it's pronounced "hy-PER-bo-lee," and it just means "exaggeration."

Was I making mountains out of molehills? Was I stretching or embroidering the truth? Was I letting my emotions run away with me?

Or was it true that Wallis was sucking up to my mother, creeping into my life like an invasive species, and that my mother thought my very existence was a horrible and humiliating mistake?

That night at dinner my mother and Wallis chattered away like best friends while I shoveled my food into my mouth and then went to bed early. The next day I gave up shelving the books. What was the point? I might as well shut myself in my room like a hermit, listening to music and waiting for my mother to come home and announce that Wallis was going to live with us forever.

I kept my earphones on and my bedroom door closed, which is why I didn't notice that Wallis was leaving. Maybe she knocked on my door to say goodbye, but I didn't hear her. I only knew she was taking off because I looked out the window and saw a small white truck pulling into the drive. I assumed the driver was just turning around, but then I saw Wallis scuttling into the passenger side.

I pushed the curtain out of the way and pressed myself against the window. Was that Wallis's mother? When the truck pulled out I barely got a glimpse of her, a dark-haired, pale, petite woman driving quickly away.

Though I felt sort of slimy while I did it, I sent a celebratory text to CeeCee and Jill. *Wallis gone at last,* I said. Glancing at the clock and seeing that CeeCee would be done with summer school in twenty minutes, I also suggested— even though she had ignored me for several days—that she and her mother might want to pick me up on their way to the pool.

Relieved to have the house to myself again, I went into the kitchen and spread some cream cheese and marmalade on a bagel. The trick to bagels, I had discovered, was in not allowing blobs of cream cheese—or worse, marmalade, which was very sticky—to escape through the hole.

No answer from Jill, but I got a text from CeeCee. *No can do,* she said. *The fam and I are leaving town.*

Going where? I asked her.

Beach.

I wondered if it would occur to her to invite me. I stared at my phone while devouring my bagel: apparently not.

I picked up my laptop and my book club book—only two more meetings and the Literary Punishment Guild would be over—and went out to the porch.

Jill was right about *The House on Mango Street*, I thought: it was short but you had to absorb it slowly, as if you were sipping its tiny chapters through a straw. I read the first few pages several times, pushing my way through the printed words until they disappeared.

Esperanza, the main character, wanted a house. She wanted a *real house* with *running water and pipes that worked. And inside it would have real stairs, not hallway stairs, but stairs inside like the houses on TV.*

I licked a dollop of cream cheese from the back of my hand and felt the words planting themselves inside me. I had a house with stairs (to the basement and the attic) and running water, but I still felt the tug of Esperanza's wanting, a wish for an unnameable *something* I had been denied.

I probably should have been nicer to Wallis. I should at least have said goodbye to her. Why had she changed her last name? It made sense for her mother to change her last name, but wouldn't Wallis have kept hers?

Never mind: I went back to the book. Esperanza's name, in Spanish, meant "hope." She was named for her great-grandmother but wanted *to baptize myself under a new name, a name more like the real me, the one nobody sees.*

I wondered what name I would choose if I renamed myself. Who would I be if I wasn't A. Haus? I opened my laptop and checked a website of baby names. Under *Adrienne* there were three different listings:

1) Adrienne: French form of Adria
2) Adria: feminine form of Adrian
3) Adrian: a famous Latin name of unknown
   meaning

Unknown meaning, I thought. That was me.

I went back to *The House on Mango Street.* Jill had said she thought one of the characters was being abused. Who was it? I finished my bagel and texted Jill again but she still didn't answer.

CeeCee's name, Cecille, meant "blind" in Latin, according to the baby name guide. Jill's name meant "sweetheart." *Wallis* wasn't listed under girls' names, but under boys' names it was defined as "Welshman" or "foreigner." I pictured Wallis, with her skinny marionette's jointed limbs, holding a bagpipe and dressed in a kilt.

There was a smear of cream cheese on my keyboard. I wiped it off and typed *Unbearable Book Club* and checked CeeCee's blog. She had made a few changes: Jill's stick-figure icon was now linked to a beef-processing plant, and I was listed as "in a relationship with an alien." And there were several new pictures—one of Jill reading *The Left Hand of Darkness* at the snack bar, one of Wallis (CeeCee must have taken it without her noticing), and one of me at the pool with my eyes half closed. My hair looked horrific— as if I had borrowed it from a woodchuck. (*Not very flattering,* my mother had told my aunt in her email.) When I clicked on my photo a caption appeared: *Will you be my dad?* Under Wallis's photo were the words *Teach me to swim!*

My mother sent me a text, asking if Wallis had left.

Yes, I said.

And are you still crabby? she asked.

I didn't answer. Let her think what she wanted. But a minute later I remembered something and sent her another text: *We need marmalade w/extra orange peel.*

Will convey asap to my personal shopper, my mother said.

Back on Mango Street again, Esperanza described the smell of her mother's hair. She paid another girl five dollars to be her friend.

"Pathetic," I said. But I could imagine, when I was younger, doing the very same thing.

I am always Esperanza, Esperanza said.

I stopped and read the line again. I didn't feel like I was "always Adrienne." CeeCee was probably always CeeCee and Jill was always Jill and Wallis was Wallis. Though I wasn't Catholic like Esperanza, I sometimes wished I could feel my own soul buried inside me, as small and undistinguished as a grain of rice.

I checked my phone. Where the heck was Jill? I decided to call her at her parents' number. She picked up. "Hey. Why are you at home today?" I asked.

"I live here," she said.

"But you aren't at work. And you haven't been answering your cell."

"That's because I didn't want to talk to you."

"Oh." This struck me as somewhat unwelcoming. "Wallis left. Can you come over?"

"No, I can't," Jill said. "I'm grounded."

"Really? Ha. You always think I'm grounded. And now you're grounded. That's kind of funny."

"Hilarious," Jill said; then she hung up the phone.

Because she wouldn't pick up after that, I had no choice but to haul my bike out of the garage, remove the cobwebs from its spokes, and travel the mile and a half to Jill's by pedaling uphill with one leg. The sun blazed overhead, relentless. My tires clung to the asphalt, which was oozing tar at the seams.

"What happened?" I asked when Jill answered the door. I noticed that she kept the screen latched between us. "You're not allowed to have visitors?" A slow-motion avalanche of frigid air was cascading toward me. "What the heck did you do?"

"Nothing," Jill said.

"Okay. Well, I just dragged my handicapped self over here in ninety-degree weather to find out why you're grounded. Can I at least have some water? When you showed up at my house I fed you sausages."

Slowly, as if moving her hands took a lot of effort, Jill unlatched the screen. "I'm letting you in because I feel sorry for you."

"How very generous," I said.

I followed Jill to the kitchen, where she filled two smiley-face glasses with water; then we went to her room. "I'm not technically grounded," she said. "I grounded myself. It kills my mother to have to punish me, so I make things easier for her by taking matters into my own hands."

This made an odd kind of sense, because it was Jill.

I gulped down my water and looked around at her room, which was totally pink. There was a pink rug, a pink quilt on the bed, a pink beanbag chair, and a row of teddy bears on a shelf. The bears were arranged in size order, and they were wearing an assortment of pink raincoats, tutus, aprons, shorts, and shoes. "Nice bears," I said.

Jill scooped up the largest in the row of animals, took off its pink plastic rain boots, and then put them back on.

"So: are you going to tell me why you grounded yourself?" I asked.

Jill licked her finger and cleaned the bear's black plastic eyes. "You don't actually know? Can you guess?"

"Why should I guess?" I asked. "Is your bedroom always this neat?"

Jill put the bear down. "Actually, I don't think I should talk about it. I don't want to be accused of spreading gossip."

"I rode all the way over here," I said. "If you don't want to say why you're grounded, can you write it down? Send smoke signals? Or maybe you want to act it out."

Jill picked up a Magic 8 Ball from her shelf. "It has to do with something that's missing." She shook the 8 Ball, a little violently I thought, then turned it over and peered into the tiny inky window. "The 8 Ball says, 'Maybe Adrienne has heard something about the thing that's missing but doesn't want to admit it.'"

"That must be in very small print," I said. "I didn't know 8 Balls were that specific."

"Oh, sure. They can tell you lots of things," Jill said. She shook the 8 Ball again, accidentally smacking it against her dresser. "Now it says, 'Adrienne has been acting like a suck-up all summer.' And it says that CeeCee is a snake—'a venomous, two-faced, treacherous beast.'"

"That's kind of over-the-top," I said. "Are you exaggerating?"

Jill said she wasn't.

"Then maybe you're reading the messages wrong. Or misinterpreting." I grabbed the 8 Ball. I shook it, then pounded it several times on the floor. "Huh," I said. "Look at this. Now the little window says that Jill D'Amato should unpack that truckload of shit from her ears and listen to me for half a second, because I have no idea what she's talking about."

"I think you cracked it," Jill said.

"Good. You're too old for an 8 Ball."

"I still have a Ouija board," Jill said. She ran her finger along a seam in the 8 Ball, which did appear to be leaking. She tossed it into the trash. "Have you ever stolen anything?" she asked.

"Like what?" I touched the earring at the top of my ear.

"Not counting accidental thievery," Jill said. "That was CeeCee, not you."

I quickly shuffled through my mental "Crimes of Adrienne" file, the list of boneheaded moments, idiotic remarks, and regrets. "I stole a bag of cashews once," I said. "I was in first grade." I remembered lifting the blue plastic package from its metal arm on the revolving display and quietly tucking it under my shirt. When my mother and I left the store, I assumed she would find the cashews and be shocked, and she would lead me back to the store to confess. But she never found them. They were delicious. "And I took a chocolate milk from the school cafeteria. I think that lunch lady, Denise, is blind in one eye."

"She's blind in both eyes," Jill said. "But I'm not talking about milk and cashews. I'm talking about expensive things. Things that are stolen from people you know. You wouldn't, for example, walk into my house and steal something valuable from my parents. You wouldn't steal my dad's medication."

"What kind of medication?" I asked, as if I might have happily stolen one type but not another.

Jill raked her fingers through her hair. "My dad needs those pills, Adrienne. It's not a joke. When he doesn't have them he feels like his nerve endings have been set on fire. And they're really expensive. You should have seen my mom's face when she found out they were gone. And nobody has been to our house since we hosted book club."

"Book club?" I asked. "But no one in the Unbearable Literary Society would steal your father's pills. No one would comb through someone else's—" I heard my voice slowing down. I remembered CeeCee checking the medicine chests.

Jill plucked a piece of fuzz off the carpet. "I know what you're thinking," she said. "And neither one of us has even mentioned her name."

"But—" I was confused. I felt like my brain had been cut loose from its usual mooring and was sloshing back and forth in my skull, like a fish in a tub.

"I've taken the shit out of my ears now," Jill said. "But I don't hear you saying anything."

"I don't have anything to say," I said. "CeeCee wouldn't have taken them."

"Why not? Do you think being a member of a book club makes her a good person?"

"I don't know," I said. It wasn't doing much for *my* moral character. "Did you at least *ask* her if she stole the pills?"

"You are a class-A idiot," Jill said. "She's not going to admit it. I asked her to come over here and talk. I said it was important, but she went to the beach."

"But . . . why are you mad at *me*?" I asked. "I didn't do anything."

"Yes, you did. You started this book club."

"I didn't start it," I said. "And I didn't steal your father's pills."

Downstairs, we heard a door close.

"That's my mom," Jill said. She tilted the pink plastic wastebasket so we could see inside it. The 8 Ball continued to leak.

"None of this makes sense to me," I said. "And I still don't understand why you're grounded. Does your mother think *you* took the pills?"

"No. Hold this. I'll get some tissues." Jill handed me the wastebasket. "The thing is, I told my mother I could guess where the pills might have gone, because I'd seen someone poking through the medicine chest. And my mom started crying. She's very sensitive. So I told her I would talk to a couple of 'suspects,' and I might be able to get the pills back. Now she probably thinks I loaned them out, or . . . I don't know what she thinks."

"Jilly, honey? Are you upstairs?"

"In my room," Jill called.

"So, basically," I said as we listened to her mother's approaching footsteps, "you told your mom that Wallis or CeeCee or I—one of the three of us—stole your dad's medication."

Jill shrugged.

"That doesn't strike you as unfair?" I asked. I thought about hiding under the bed or in the closet. But the door opened and there I was, red-handed, holding a dripping wastebasket over the rug.

Jill's mother held out her arms. Not sure what the proper response should be, I set the wastebasket down and let her press me to her chest.

"It's so good to see you, Adrienne!" she said. "That's very sweet of you to visit. We don't see enough of you, outside of book club. How's your mother? And how's little Wallis?"

"Everyone's fine. It's good to see you, too," I said.

Her eyes thickened with tears. "Well. Can I make you two something to eat? Adrienne, honey, can you stay for dinner?"

"No, I should get going," I said.

Jill's mother squeezed me again. "Oh! You girls. I know we'll survive all these challenges, won't we? You're still so young!"

"Mom? You should let go of Adrienne," Jill said.

Her mother nodded and dabbed at her eyes. "I'm fairly emotional these days. Jilly can tell you. Maybe it's all this literature we're reading. Some of it is so powerful!" She picked up *The House on Mango Street*. "Where do you think these writers get their ideas?"

I said I didn't know.

"Well, I certainly hope they aren't all true," Jill's mother said. "Some of the characters go through such terrible things. It's just . . . upsetting. What do you think, Jilly?"

Jill patted her mother's arm. She suggested that writers might be an unusual group, and that more well-adjusted people—people like us—probably kept busy with work and hobbies and didn't feel a need to write anything down.

• • • • • • • • • • •

14. ANTAGONIST: the character who is against the main character. The monster is Frankenstein's antagonist. The husband in "The Yellow Wallpaper" is the antagonist of his wife. I don't know if most people in real life have antagonists, but everyone in a novel seems to have at least one.

In books, it's never the obvious person who's guilty. The person who's found standing over the corpse with a bloodstained weapon in her hand almost never turns out to be the killer. The killer is the person you would never think of, the one who wandered through the second chapter in a friendly way, or the person who—up until the minute she confesses—wouldn't seem to be capable of the simplest crime.

I didn't think CeeCee stole the pills.

Did she? Maybe anything was possible. Maybe my mother was lying to me, and maybe Wallis's mother was a figment of my imagination, and maybe CeeCee had ransacked Jill's bathroom cabinet so she could steal the pills for someone who would know how to sell them—let's say an unemployed guy who liked to run errands at three a.m.

CeeCee wasn't answering my texts. Was that incriminating? Or did it just mean she was tired of me? I checked her blog. It didn't seem to have changed, but I saw a number 44 in the *Post a comment* section. Forty-four comments? Who would bother to comment on a book club blog?

Oh.

Hey CeeCee, great blog, most of them said. *I like the bikini.* One person asked about my hair (*Does that chick have a mullett?*) and several people sent links—these were probably obscene—that CeeCee might want to use for her project. One person offered to be *the daddy I had always wanted.*

Nice. A pedophile.

The last few comments were from Jeff Pardullo. *Hot,* he said, commenting on the picture of CeeCee's toes. In another post he wrote, *Call me. I wanna hang out with your high school friends.*

I wondered if Jill or Wallis had seen the comments. Then it occurred to me that Wallis, who didn't even want her picture taken, probably didn't know about the blog at all.

CeeCee finally reappeared a couple of days later, on the morning of Unbearable Book Club meeting number four. I woke up to find her sitting at the foot of my bed with a clock in her hand.

"What are you doing?" I asked.

She held the face of the clock in my direction.

"Nine-forty-five," she said. "Is this when you non–summer school students usually get up?"

"How did you get in here?" I rubbed my eyes. "And why aren't you at French?"

"Your front door was unlocked." CeeCee put the clock down. "Very low security. And I'm here because my mother made me get up hideously early this morning and drive back from the beach so I could get to class, but Monsieur Crowne didn't show—*il est malade.* So I had my mom drop me off at your house on her way to tennis. Can you make cappuccino?"

"I don't even know what it is," I said. The sun was pouring through my bedroom window. I peeled the sheet from my legs. "Do you know I called you about twenty times?"

"No. My phone died," CeeCee said. "It was some kind of Stone Age model. I'm finally getting a new one. My little vacation was pretty entertaining, by the way. Remind me to tell you about it when you're older. What beach do you usually go to?"

"I don't. My mother hates the beach," I said, sitting up. "It's a scarring memory for her, because I was born somewhere nearby."

"Parents." CeeCee shrugged. "So I noticed Wallis is gone," she said. "I'm going to award you the National Tolerance of Wacky Intruders Prize for putting up with her. How long was she here?"

"Three years," I said. "CeeCee, I need to—"

"Hang on." She cut me off. "We have book club tonight, right? Are we meeting at Wallis's?"

"No. At the pool. The picnic grounds. I need to tell you—"

"You need to brush your teeth," she said. "You're not telling me anything until you smell better."

I stared at her. "I just woke up. You *woke* me up."

"Yeah, I remember that," she said. "Hey, nice boxer shorts. But are you going to get dressed? You should try to look presentable when you have company."

I went off to brush my teeth and to pee. I asked the mirror over the bathroom sink if CeeCee would bother to show up for book club if she'd stolen the pills. The mirror told me I looked like an idiot when I talked to myself. "Thanks," I said.

Back in my room, CeeCee handed me a pair of jean shorts that looked vaguely familiar.

"Where did those come from?" I asked.

"I found them in your drawer and cut them off with your scissors. They'll look much better at this length."

"I've hardly worn those yet," I said. But I assumed she was right; there was probably a reason I hadn't worn them. I stepped into the closet to get dressed. My knee was looking better again; it was almost back to its normal size. "I wasn't the only one trying to get hold of you," I said. "Did you hear Jill was grounded?"

"For what?" CeeCee asked. "Memorizing too many vocabulary words?"

I put on a pair of flip-flops and a shirt and stepped out of the closet. "Somebody stole her dad's medication."

With her back to me, CeeCee was unscrewing a lip-gloss container she had found on my dresser.

"It was a bunch of pills," I said. "Did you know they were missing?"

She stuck her pinky into the lip gloss. "Why are you asking me that?"

I looked in the mirror. "These do look good as shorts," I said.

Without turning around, CeeCee asked, "Is Jill saying I stole her father's pills?"

"Yeah, kind of," I said. "She's been consulting an 8 Ball and a Ouija board."

CeeCee opened the top drawer of my dresser and riffled through it. "I guess it would make things easier for her if I stole them," she said. "It's always nice to have a bad person to point to. Someone who's guilty. What's the word for that? Like a kind of enemy."

"Scapegoat?" I asked.

She opened a little wooden box and examined my shark tooth collection and my stack of silver dollars. "You think I stole them, too," she said.

I paused for a second before I answered. "You didn't pick up when Jill tried to ask you about it," I said. "And we saw you going through the medicine cabinets. I wondered if Jeff . . ." My thoughts were tangled. "Why is he on your blog? And you have to take those captions down; I've got some kind of pedophile asking if he can be my dad."

"You said 'we.'" CeeCee closed the lid of the wooden box. "*We* saw you. Do you know what's interesting?"

"What?"

She turned around. "I saved your butt that night you got drunk," she said. "I cleaned your vomit out of Jeff's car."

"You did? Sorry, I wasn't—"

"And you never said anything about it. You got wasted and passed out and had to be rescued but you're still the good girl," she said. "I'm the one who's a thief."

"I told Jill you didn't steal the pills," I said. "Go ahead and ask her. But the evidence makes you look guilty." We stared at each other. "And Jill's mother probably thinks you did it. So you might not want to come to book club."

"Thanks for the tip," CeeCee said. "But my attendance record is perfect. I'd hate to miss a meeting." She noticed my copy of *The House on Mango Street* on my desk. "That's the new one?" she asked.

I said it was.

She picked up the book and read the back cover.

"Listen," I said. "I'll talk to Jill before the meeting. I'll tell her—"

"Don't worry about it," CeeCee said. "What are . . . *vine*—hang on—*vignettes?*"

I looked over her shoulder at the book. "Little pieces," I said. "It's French."

"And what's *so-delate?*" She put her finger under the word.

"*Desolate,*" I said. "You read it wrong."

She held out the book. "Are you going to read it to me?"

I looked at the thick blue type on the back cover. "You're dyslexic," I said.

"Yeah, whatever. Reading gives me a headache."

"That's why you always want me to read to you. Maybe you should get glasses."

"I don't want glasses."

"But how will you—"

"You don't have to read if you don't want to," CeeCee said. "It's not a big deal."

I opened the book. She sat on the bed, near the window, looking out through the screen. I read to her about Esperanza and the things that she wanted; then I read about a character named Marin, who dances to a radio under a streetlight, *waiting for a car to stop, a star to fall, someone to change her life.*

"Pitiful," CeeCee said. But I knew she was waiting for me to keep going.

I read a little bit more and then skipped a few chapters. I read about Esperanza getting a job and about her grandfather dying. Later, at an amusement park with a friend, Esperanza meets a guy who presses himself against her. She describes *his dirty fingernails against my skin.* I felt a tingling at the back of my neck.

"You should take the comments section out of the blog," I said.

"Don't worry about Jeff," CeeCee said. "Have you kissed him yet?"

"No. But I don't think other people should read about us," I said. "At least you should take down our pictures. I hate the one you took of me. And Wallis didn't want her picture taken." I remembered the scar on Wallis's forehead. She had changed her last name. *His dirty fingernails against my skin.*

"Oh, shit," I said.

CeeCee was brushing her hair. "What?"

Jill had told me that *someone in the book was being abused.*

My mother thought I was *impressionable*, but what if Wallis—

"You have to take down the blog," I said. "It isn't safe."

"Nobody cares about blogs," CeeCee said.

"I'll read you all five of the books. And I'll help you come up with a different project."

She put her hairbrush back in her purse. "I'll get rid of the comments section," she said.

"Can you make the blog private?" I asked. "So only the four of us can see it?"

"Yeah, I guess so," she said. "Read me some more of the book, and I'll work on the blog this afternoon."

I was anxious and jittery that night when my mother and I left for book club. "Why are you tapping your fingers like that?" my mother asked. "Are you worried about something?"

"Me?" I asked, as if—though we were alone in the car—my mother might be talking to somebody else. I had checked the blog and was relieved to see that the comments section was gone; still, I had a few lingering concerns about the evening ahead of us. For example, would Jill's mother have CeeCee hauled away in handcuffs? Would Wallis's mother suddenly show up and take one look at me and say, "That's the inebriated girl I almost accidentally killed"?

When we got to the picnic grounds, Wallis was spreading a plastic cloth on one of the tables. My mother had brought paper plates and cups; Wallis had brought a bottle of soda, a pair of salt and pepper shakers, and two cookie tins.

Sitting down at one end of the splintery bench, I noticed the row of metal rings on the tablecloth. "Is this an old shower curtain?" I asked.

My mother raised her eyebrows in my direction. I could smell the chlorine and hear shrieks and splashing from the pool.

"I made hard-boiled eggs," Wallis announced in her growly voice. "And I brought carrot sticks and I filled pieces of celery with peanut butter. And added raisins." She took the lid off a cookie tin. "Here are the eggs."

I noticed the stale crumbs of ginger snaps or graham crackers around the lid of the tin.

Jill and her mother parked near the swings and walked slowly toward us. When they reached the table, Jill's mother fussed over Wallis's culinary skills.

I had texted Jill an hour earlier to give her a heads-up that CeeCee was coming. *Brace yourself,* she texted back. Now she avoided looking in my direction. She was eating an orange Popsicle; a bee circled her wrist.

In various cities and towns across the country, I thought, people were gathering on porches and around tables and on comfortable sofas to exchange ideas about books. They would probably discuss the lives of the characters, who were always more interesting than real-life people, and point to the parts of the stories they liked best. I had a feeling our discussion would be somewhat different.

CeeCee and her mother got out of their car, both of them wearing dark glasses; they crossed the parking lot together on two sets of matching, elegant legs and sat next to each other at the end of the bench. Jill's orange Popsicle crumbled into several pieces and was lost in the grass.

Not realizing what she was up against, my mother tried to kick-start a discussion. She got CeeCee's mother to agree that *The House on Mango Street* was short. And that it was hard to tell who some of the characters were at first, because there were so many of them.

I scraped some orange soap scum from the tablecloth and looked at Jill.

Silence.

My mother observed that this was the first contemporary, realistic title that our group had read, the first book to deal with the concrete dangers, for people our age, of sex and drugs. She wondered what CeeCee and Jill and Wallis and I thought of it.

"Egg?" CeeCee asked. She passed me the tin, the boiled eggs sliding around inside it. Some of them had pieces of grass stuck to them.

"Thanks." I took an egg.

Jill's mother cleared her throat and said she thought the portrayal of the social problems in the book was very important, because drugs and violence and dishonesty happened everywhere, even among people we knew. She glanced at CeeCee. "Even here in West New Hope," she said.

The egg tasted odd. Biting into its rubbery surface, I detected a subtle whiff of chlorine, as if Wallis had peeled and rinsed it in the pool.

CeeCee's mother said she hadn't finished the book yet

but that kids like Esperanza grew up too fast, and kids in the inner cities in particular—

"Celerypeanutbutterandraisin?" CeeCee asked.

I took a piece of celery but disposed of the raisins, which are basically spoiled fruit. The carrots, rolling around in the same tin, were knobby and misshapen and hadn't been peeled.

Jill's mother said she'd be interested to know what CeeCee's mother meant by "kids like Esperanza." Was she referring to people who weren't wealthy? People who weren't white?

CeeCee's mother took her sunglasses off. "That's a very odd question."

Blushing, Jill's mother said she was only asking because in her experience, and maybe others would not agree with her, regular middle-class and city kids weren't any worse or any different than kids in the suburbs who had grown up in supposedly "good" families, families that could easily afford—

"Oops." CeeCee squeezed one of the hard-boiled eggs, and it shot out of her fist and across the table, hitting me in the chest.

"Egg war," I said.

CeeCee's mother looked fixedly at Jill's across the table. "It sounds like you're making a point," she said. "Or an accusation."

"I might be." Jill's mother turned abruptly to CeeCee. "Did you take something that belongs to us?" she asked.

CeeCee selected a carrot from the cookie tin. "What did you have in mind?"

"Excuse me." CeeCee's mother put her hand between them. "Are you suggesting my daughter stole something?"

"Mom," Jill said. "We can—"

"Jilly, I'm just asking a question. I'd like to know," her mother said.

"And I asked *you* a question." CeeCee's mother leaned across the shower curtain. "You have an awful lot of nerve."

My mother tried to intercede. "This is silly," she said. "We should talk this out, and not make accusations."

CeeCee's mother stood up. "I don't think it's *silly*. And if anyone's accusing people of stealing, I'd like to point out that Adrienne is wearing my diamond earring, which has been missing for almost a month."

"Adrienne is *what*?" My mother turned to stare at me. "Is that a real diamond?"

"I didn't know it was real," I said. "It's pretty big."

"You didn't know it was real but you stole it?" my mother asked.

I looked down at the damp spot on my shirt where the egg had hit me. "That's right," I said. "I've been meaning to tell you. I broke into CeeCee's house one night. I put on my black ski mask and my burglar shoes, and I climbed the stairs and opened the door to her parents' bedroom and found her mother's jewelry box. And when I looked through her jewelry I decided to steal this single earring." I saw Jill shake her head. "I'm not sure why I did it," I went on. "It must have been the influence of this book club. Now that you've caught me, I'll give it back." I grabbed the

180

diamond in front, pinched the fastener at the back of my ear (some of my skin had grown over it), and wrenched out the stud. "Here." I put the fastener and the diamond on a paper plate in front of CeeCee's mother. There was a piece of skin stuck to it. "Thanks for the loan."

Without even thinking about where I was headed, I found my flip-flops slapping against my feet. They carried me across the dusty grass of the picnic grounds and through the pool gate (the ticket taker was gone) and across the squelchy red rubber mat that led to the cave of the locker room.

Jill was behind me. "That was unusual," she said. "For what it's worth, I asked my mother not to make a scene."

"I guess she decided not to listen to you," I said.

"I guess not. Your ear is bleeding." Jill knocked on a door to one of the toilets. "Anyone home?" All the stall doors were crooked: they hung like slips of misaligned paper on a bulletin board. Jill unfurled some toilet paper and told me to press it against my ear.

"The good news," I said, "is that we only have one more meeting."

Someone flushed a toilet. An older woman in a flowered bathing suit emerged from a stall and washed her hands at the sink. She glared at us—*Teenagers!*—and then lumbered off to the towel dispenser.

"CeeCee didn't take the pills," I said.

Jill took a deep breath through her nose, then let it out. "Nothing that's happened in this book club makes any sense," she said. "I miss being in school. I wish we could have torn some pages out of the calendar and gone straight from June to September. Oh, God, here she comes."

"Hello, literary friends." CeeCee sauntered around the corner near the shower room. She stopped by the sinks. Though the mirrors above them were bolted to the wall, CeeCee pretended to open one. "Let's see," she said. "Oh, a tweezer for my collection. I obviously want that. And a used toothbrush and a dirty sponge, *check*. And a thermometer—I hope it's not rectal. And here's my favorite nail polish." She pretended to unscrew a lid and paint her nails. A little girl in a two-piece bathing suit paused by the toilets, mesmerized.

"I didn't tell my mother you stole them," Jill said. "I let her come to her own conclusions."

CeeCee was still painting her nails with the invisible brush.

"You did the same thing," Jill said. "You let your mother think Adrienne stole her earring."

"That's true," I said.

"That was a joke. It was funny," said CeeCee.

I pressed another wad of tissue to my ear.

"Well, I'm glad you've got a sense of humor," Jill said. "Because my dad's missing medication is pretty hilarious. It's almost as funny as your mother's racist statements about 'city kids' being the only ones who do drugs."

"My mom's not a racist," CeeCee said.

Jill turned to me. "I don't know if you've heard—I hope it's just an ugly rumor—that there are Asians moving into West New Hope."

"Thanks for the warning. We'll be on the lookout," CeeCee said.

A voice on the PA system announced that the pool was going to close in ten minutes.

"Thanks for taking the comments down," I told CeeCee.

I explained to Jill that CeeCee was going to make the book blog private. "So we won't have wackos all over the country who can look at our pictures or find out where we live."

"You can't get rid of the pictures," Jill said. "Someone's already copied them. They're all over."

"What do you mean?"

She shook her head. "Have you heard of the *World Wide Web*? Even if CeeCee gets rid of the blog, the pictures are out there." She struck a pose. "*Will you be my dad?* It even says that you live in West New Hope."

"But—"

"And it's not just you," Jill said. "Wallis is the one who didn't want her picture taken. Has she seen it? *Teach me to swim?*"

Wallis appeared in the locker room doorway. "What pictures are you talking about?" she asked.

The Awakening

15. EPIPHANY: Probably because I once saw my third-grade teacher use an EpiPen, driving the point of it into Jordan Wersall, who'd been stung by a bee, I think of an epiphany as something that gets injected into the main character so she suddenly sees things differently.

The Involuntary Book Club for Intolerable Girls was disbanded. Jill's mother and CeeCee's weren't speaking. Wallis had walked home by herself, and Jill's mother had driven away from the picnic grounds in tears. Because we were the last ones to leave, my mother and I had folded up the mildewy shower curtain and thrown out the leftover food and tossed the cookie tins into the back of our car. At home, we had a stimulating conversation about stolen diamonds and missing pills.

I didn't tell her what my suspicions were about Wallis. I was generally wrong about everything, and I didn't trust myself anymore. Besides, at the pool, when CeeCee and

Jill and I had told her about the blog, Wallis hadn't seemed horrified or upset; she had stood with her feet splayed in a puddle of slimy water, blinking at nothing. Jill had ended up almost sticking up for CeeCee: the blog was mainly a joke, she explained—something CeeCee had made up as a half-serious fulfillment of Ms. Radcliffe's assignment. There were pictures, she said, and someone had copied them and emailed and posted them here and there, but—

"What are the pictures of?" Wallis asked.

"They're of us," I said. "The Unbearable Girls. But they aren't inappropriate. I mean, you look nice."

This was a substantial exaggeration: in one of her photos, Wallis was holding up her arm to block the camera; in another, she was out of focus and frowzy, a copy of *The House on Mango Street* in her hand.

Mr. Geertz, the pool manager, had stuck his head through the doorway and announced that he was locking up. "No hanging around here after dark, girls," he said.

The four of us filed out of the locker room and walked toward the fence. Through the gate, in the picnic grounds, I could see our mothers shouting at each other around the table.

Jill's mother blew her nose and waved, her hand over her head like a drowning victim, then ran to her car.

"That's my signal, I guess," Jill said.

"I just wish they could behave themselves and be more mature." CeeCee sighed. We headed toward the picnic table. Halfway there, I turned around to say something to Wallis—something about the fact that she could talk to us

185

if she was worried about the pictures, that she could confide in us, and trust us. But Wallis was gone.

It was a relief, being done with the book club. No more conflict, no more intrigue, no more drama. Now I could read the last book on my own. I didn't need to discuss it with anyone, did I? Besides, Jill was busy at work, and Wallis was probably hibernating out in the woods, and CeeCee's mother and mine weren't on very good terms, which meant I had lost my ride to the pool. For three or four days I stayed home by myself and watched pointless TV, and—even though she had given up asking me to do it—I finished alphabetizing and shelving my mother's books.

The house was quiet when I finished with Wolfe, Woolf, Yep, Yezierska, Zusak. I checked my phone for any messages (nope) from the Unbearable Girls. Wandering into the kitchen, I heard the dishwasher finish its cycle, the pipes clearing their throats.

At the end of Cisneros's novel, Esperanza writes, *One day I will go away. Friends and neighbors will say, What happened to that Esperanza? Where did she go with all those books and paper?*

I didn't think anyone would say that about me. They would say, "Adrienne? Did she used to live here?"

After foraging around for a few minutes, I opened an economy-sized bag of potato chips and made some iced tea. On the other side of the bay window, sweating people moved slowly through a thick green world.

The mail came. I went out to collect it. In the rhododendrons to the right of the mailbox, Mr. Finkle was reluctantly completing a late-morning kill. His fur was as glossy and striking as CeeCee's hair, which made me briefly imagine CeeCee as an enormous feline, batting a miniature Jeff around with her velvet paws. "Scat," I said.

I reached into the mailbox, which was hot enough to cook potatoes in, and found the usual collection of catalogs and junk. And at the bottom of the pile, a letter in a small blue envelope, addressed to me. I tore it open.

Dear Adrienne. I enjoyed being friends with you this summer. I enjoyed being in the Book Bondage Unbearable Literary Enslavement Club. Thank you for including me. We are leaving West New Hope soon. Goodbye.
                                                    —Wallis

I read the letter two or three times. A needle of guilt stitched its way through my chest.

I hadn't wanted to be a member of a book club. I hadn't wanted to meet once a week and discuss the books on our list—but now that I had they were taking up space inside me; they had staked out parcels of land in my brain. And I hadn't wanted to hang around with CeeCee and Wallis and Jill, but that's what I had done. Though I still found her creepy, Wallis was a part of the story that wasn't over. She was . . .

As if waiting to sneeze, I knew I was about to understand something. I was about to experience a realization.

I called Jill at the pool. "I think I'm having an epiphany," I said.

"That sounds painful," Jill said. "But who's this? Is this

a member of the book club I used to belong to? The one that doesn't exist anymore?"

"We still exist," I said. "That's part of the epiphany. Did you hear that Wallis and her mother are moving?"

"That'll be two-fifty," Jill said. She was working the snack bar again.

I read her Wallis's note. "Do you think she's moving because of the pictures? I mean, the blog?"

"Probably not. She and her mother were only renting. I don't think they were ever planning to stay. Hey, tank suit," Jill said. "Soda's a dollar. An American dollar. I don't want any more of those Canadian coins."

"I feel kind of bad about it," I said. "This seems really sudden."

"It only seems sudden because you didn't know. Maybe they were always planning to leave."

"But maybe they weren't," I said. "Are you busy tonight?"

"Um, definitely," Jill said. "Since you're the one asking."

"Okay, tomorrow night. That's better anyway. My mother won't be here. She's having dinner with a friend in Philadelphia. I'll call CeeCee and Wallis."

"Wait a minute. You want to have a book club meeting?" Jill asked.

I heard the sound of coins spilling into the cash box. "We haven't finished the books yet," I said.

"So?"

"So we need to finish them. We have to meet." *Though we never intended to be a group,* I thought, *that's what we've become.*

188

"You're not doing anything else tomorrow," I said. "Come over at seven. I'll make you something to eat."

"Look, Kevin or whoever you are. Kevin's brother. Wait in line," Jill said. "I'm not going to sell you anything if you can't wait your turn."

"Jill?" I asked.

"Yeah, okay," she said. "My parents are going out for their anniversary tomorrow. But I probably won't tell them I'm hanging out with you. You and CeeCee aren't at the top of my mother's list right now."

"I thought your mother liked me," I said. "I'm not at the bottom of her list, am I?"

"You're probably somewhere in the middle," Jill said. "It's a pretty short list. And God and my dad and my grandma are on it. I have to sign off. Lots of customers here." She put her phone down but forgot to press Off. Listening to the noise of the pool in the background—the shouting, the whistling, the general commotion—I thought, *I am a lonely person. That's why I read books.*

That night after dinner it was my turn to do the dishes, but I put it off because my mother was in the kitchen, cleaning out cabinets and talking to my aunt Beatrice on the phone. My mother and I had been polite to each other since the blowout at the picnic grounds, but we hadn't talked. Maybe she was waiting for me to apologize. But I'd begun to lose track of the many things I was supposed to be sorry for, and had begun to think that instead of apologizing, I should just get older and move away so that she would realize, at least in hindsight, what an appealing person I'd been.

189

I went out to the porch to let her talk. Though I wasn't sure anyone else would read it, I lay down on the wicker sofa with book club selection number five: *The Awakening.* The air was heavy and still, and I could just hear the up-and-down of my mother's voice when I turned the first pages.

Edna Pontellier was crying because her husband said she was a lousy mother. Later he tried to make up for being nasty by buying her chocolates. Edna was rich but unsatisfied and moody. She was on vacation, and it was hot, and she spent most of her time resting or strolling or "bathing" in the sea—even though she was terrified of the water. *An ungovernable dread hung about her* because she couldn't swim.

I felt myself dipping beneath the surface. "Adrienne?" Mrs. Pontellier was offering me a chocolate. She was asking me to walk along the path with her, to the gulf. She was going to lend me her sunshade and her pretty dogskin gloves.

"Adrienne."

"What?" I said. "I'm reading."

"With your eyes shut?" my mother asked. "You're falling asleep reading *The Awakening.* That seems ironic."

"Are you waking me up to demonstrate irony?" I asked.

"No, I'm waking you up because it's getting late. I'm going to bed. And I wanted to remind you to do the dishes."

"I know." I stood up. "I was waiting for you to get off the phone."

"I also wanted to remind you," my mother said, "since

you'll probably be asleep when I leave for work tomorrow, that I'm going to dinner with my friend Melissa in Philadelphia. I won't be home until after eleven."

"Yup." I nodded, staggering into the kitchen while my mother locked the door to the porch. In the kitchen sink, I found our dishes submerged in several inches of greasy water.

"And one other thing," my mother said. She had followed me back to the kitchen. "I was just talking to your aunt Beatrice."

I took the two pots out of the sink and set them aside.

"And she was wondering . . . well, she's invited you to come to Atlanta."

I tried to extract the silverware from under the plates. "Atlanta? It's probably hotter there than it is here."

"That might be true. But Aunt Beatrice has air-conditioning," my mother said. Before I could point out that it would be cheaper for me to stay home and leave the air conditioner on in our own house than it would be to buy a round-trip ticket to Georgia, my mother said, "This has been a hard summer, Adrienne."

"Hard," I said, staring into the sink.

"*Stressful* is probably a better word," my mother said. "I've been working a lot, and you've been home on your own, and it just seemed to your aunt and me . . ."

A ticker-tape machine in my head started printing out messages, all of which drowned my mother out. *She wants you out of the house. She was willing to put up with you when you were little and cute, but not now, with your knee in a brace and a scab*

191

on your ear and a drinking problem. Instead of sending you back to school in the fall, she's going to ship you off to a reeducation camp or a prison farm.

I found a scouring pad, like a slimy silver wig for a fish, and scrubbed at the islands of burned rice at the bottom of a pot.

"Do you have any thoughts?" my mother asked.

"About what?" I said.

"About what I just said." My mother leaned against the counter. "Adrienne, I know I've asked you this already, but I'm asking again: You don't know where these pills are? The ones that went missing from the D'Amatos' house?"

I said I did not.

"And you aren't taking drugs of any kind? You aren't taking pills?"

"I am not ingesting pills or other substances," I said. "I completed the drug awareness program in seventh grade."

This was probably one of the times when my mother found herself wishing for a second parent: *She already lied to me about the drinking. You handle her this time, Frank.* I imagined a big-bellied, gruff, unshaven man, his arm looped like a hairy rope around my mother's shoulders. "Are you all right?" my mother asked.

I stared into the filthy basin of water. "Why do you hate going to the beach?"

"The beach?" My mother wiped her hands on a towel.

"It's not because you get sunburned, is it?"

"What's with the beach all of a sudden?" my mother asked.

"I'm just asking a question," I said. A greasy tsunami of tepid water splattered my shirt.

"Adrienne, are you crying?"

"Yes," I said.

"But why?" she asked.

"I asked you a question first," I said. "And you have to answer." I plunged a second pot into the sink. "I can ask you any question I want, because those are our rules."

"Okay." My mother stood close beside me. "I do get sunburned at the beach," she said. "And I do get a rash. But I also don't like going to the beach because I have . . . difficult memories of being there."

This was the word she had used in her email to my Aunt Beatrice: *difficult*. I was difficult—a difficult person. "You made mistakes there," I said.

"Mistakes?"

A tear rolled down my cheek and dropped into the sink. "You did stupid things."

My mother took a step back. "I suppose I did some stupid things when I was younger," she said. "But I still don't understand why you're crying."

Because you called me a mistake, I thought. *Because you think I'm a criminal. Because I am wrong about everything and you wish I was like Wallis, with her Rule of Three Thousand. Because I want to be a person the Quaker Oats man would know how to describe.*

"It's too hard to summarize," I said. I tried to wipe my nose on my sleeve.

My mother said she was sorry I was upset, and we could talk about a trip to Atlanta later.

"Forget it. You can tell Aunt Beatrice I'll go," I said. I

193

told myself it would be better if I left. If remnants of the blog were still floating around, I would be out of reach when all the homeless people and pedophiles lined up at the door to ask if they were my dad.

My mother took out the trash. When she came back I was in my room. She knocked on the door. "You're okay?" she asked.

I said I was.

"Call if you need me tomorrow." She paused in the hall, then turned out the light. "You'll be good while I'm gone?"

16. STREAM OF CONSCIOUSNESS: *Stream* is a metaphor, I guess. Because nobody's mind is really a stream. It just feels that way sometimes when you're sitting around doing nothing and all kinds of weird thoughts are floating through your head on their way to wherever. And some writers write this way, to show you what it's like when the stream of consciousness is flowing along in one of their characters' heads.

What did I want from the final meeting of the Excruciating Reader's Group for Abominable Girls? I wanted an ending. I wanted Wallis to talk to us and tell us the truth. I wanted Jill to admit she knew that CeeCee hadn't taken the pills. I wanted CeeCee to promise to stop hanging around with Jeff, and I wanted her to read *The Awakening* all the way through.

I thought of the speech I was going to give when they showed up. It was going to be something inspirational, something about trust and pulling through hardship as a group. I imagined my voice almost echoing as I spoke. I would talk about letting this last book unite us, one book to finally . . . I realized I was thinking about *The Fellowship of the Ring*.

I read a few more chapters of *The Awakening* before I noticed it was getting dark. It was only three-forty-five, but the sky, when I went out to the porch, was thick and gray, and it was closing down over West New Hope like the lid of a pot. I heard a tapping on the roof of the house—the sound of a giant drumming his fingers—then a pause while the wind turned a corner and the temperature, which had hovered in the nineties for almost a month, dropped by twenty degrees.

Lightning.

The thunder that followed seemed to grab hold of the sky above the house and shake it out like a rug; from inside the porch, I watched silver streams of water falling to the ground, water clotting against the screens, water rinsing the heat from the air and sliding serpentlike over the grass on its way to the street, which sent tendrils of steam up to meet it, water churning, turning the outside world into a blur, a wet green painting.

I stood and watched, getting wet through the screens. The porch felt like a ship. Thunder trembled the floor under my feet; the sky darkened and swelled. The trees, rattling their greenery and tossing their heads, were bent low to the ground.

My mother sent me a text: *Is our house still standing?*

Parts of it are, I said.

The rain fell for hours. When it finally stopped, almost

as quickly as it started, I opened the windows and doors to let the new air in. Then I went outside to look at the branches and the shingles from our neighbor's roof, littered over our lawn. I collected a stack of the shingles, along with a drainpipe and a deflated soccer ball. A few minutes later I saw Jill on her bike, riding into the driveway with a bottle of ketchup under her arm.

"You travel with condiments?" I asked.

She got off the bike and leaned it against the railing by the front steps. "Only when I'm thinking about hot dogs," she said. "Last time I was here I think I spotted a pack in your freezer. Is your power out?" She kicked at a branch that had fallen across the sidewalk.

"I don't know." I flipped the light switch by the front door: nothing.

"Yup. Powerless," Jill said. "All of West New Hope's going dark. There are a lot of trees down." We went inside.

"This is the first time all summer that I haven't been sweaty," Jill said. "I smell really good. Do you want to smell me?"

"No," I said. "Thanks."

We went into the kitchen, where Jill immediately started rummaging through the freezer. "Are these kosher?" She held up a package of frozen hot dogs.

"Don't leave the freezer open; you'll melt the ice cream," I said. "Anyway, what do you care about kosher? You aren't Jewish."

"Kosher dogs taste better," Jill said. She put a pot on the stove, then reached for the knob and realized the stove was electric. "Dang. A serious setback." She bit her lip, then stared at the frosted package in her hand. "Where are your candles? Maybe I can cook these over a flame."

"Do you think Wallis and CeeCee will show up tonight?" I asked.

"I don't know. You're the one who invited them." Jill found our junk drawer and started raking through our collection of chopsticks, tea strainers, pickle pickers, tape dispensers, batteries, pencil stubs, coasters, and glue. "Which means that, even though you keep denying it, you're still president of the book club. Chief organizer. Ooh. A flashlight. You're going to need that."

"Wallis should have told us she was leaving town," I said. I opened the cabinet above the junk drawer and handed Jill a green pine-scented candle from the previous Christmas. "Do you know where they're moving?"

"Connecticut. Her mom got a job there." Jill plopped the candle onto a plate. "Are you going to miss her?"

"Do you mean Wallis? Am I going to miss Wallis?"

"That was my question." Jill found a pack of matches and lit the candle.

I wasn't sure how to answer. Maybe that's why I had wanted to meet. Would I miss Wallis's bear-cub voice and her rashy legs and the sight of her wearing my castoff clothes?

Jill opened the hot dogs and forked them apart under running water while giving me a tally of what she had sold that week at the pool. She managed to spear one of the franks with a knife. "Somebody's knocking at your door," she said. She looked out the window over the sink. "Actually, at both doors. We're in here!" she yelled. CeeCee and Wallis had showed up at the front and back of the house, and arrived in the kitchen at the same time.

My *Fellowship of the Ring* speech, as if attached to a fistful of helium balloons, floated gently away.

"Are you cooking a hot dog over a candle?" CeeCee asked. Jill was holding a kosher frank over the pine-scented flame.

"Why not?" Jill asked. "The package says they're precooked. Hey, Wallis."

"Hi," Wallis said.

We stood around in the kitchen talking about nothing, our conversation a wandering river of aimless ideas. Jill said her parents had driven to Maryland for their anniversary. "Every year they eat at the restaurant where they had their first date, and after they eat they drive to a park where they used to make out."

CeeCee said that people over twenty-five should never make out, and then Jill told a story about a girl who'd had the hiccups for eleven years, and Wallis made some observations about meteors, which were often called shooting stars, she said, even though they weren't stars, and CeeCee wanted to know if any of us worried about getting brain cancer from our cell phones, because she had heard on the radio that they emitted the same whatever-y things as microwaves, which meant they were literally frying our brains, but Wallis said the research wasn't reliable and she hoped we understood that meteors streaked across the sky by the millions each day, in fact it would probably be easy to see them on a night like this, with the power out, particularly if we were up on a hill or a roof.

Jill had sliced up two hot dogs but they were still partly frozen, and the little pink pork cylinders, because of the candle she had used to roast them, tasted somewhat like pine. "We can get to your roof from your attic," she said. "Right?"

I said that my mother didn't want us up there.

CeeCee had found a package of marshmallows in the cabinet. She pointed to my copy of *The Awakening* on the kitchen table. "Should we bring this with us?"

We blew out the candle and left the hot dogs on the counter. I grabbed the flashlight and a beach towel that we could sit on. Then I led the way up the attic stairs and stepped through the window above my mother's bedroom and climbed onto the roof.

"This town looks better in the dark," Jill said. "It's almost pretty."

"I've heard people say that about you," CeeCee said.

Standing side by side, we could see exactly where the blackout had hit, because the lights south of West New Hope were just being turned on. Though our whole town was dark, we could pick out the landmarks: the rectangular roofs of the other houses, the meandering shape of the creek, the elementary school, the Towne Centre, and the beginning of the road that led to the park, and beyond it, to Wallis's. I felt as if I were looking at an architect's model:

I almost expected to see a tiny version of myself, living within the grid we were looking down on.

CeeCee tore the bag of marshmallows open. "I don't see any meteors, Wallis."

Wallis said we had to wait until it got darker.

I spread out the towel so we could sit down.

"Hey, Adrienne: this is a good place for your epiphany," Jill said.

"Yeah," I agreed. But I couldn't remember what my epiphany was. It had probably trickled out the bottom of my brain like a hair down a sink. Still, I thought I remembered that it had involved wanting the book club and the books we had read to have some kind of meaning. "School starts three weeks from now," I said.

"That's a lousy epiphany." CeeCee clicked the flashlight on and then off. "Do people still use Morse code?" she asked. "Did we learn it in Girl Scouts?"

Jill reminded her that she'd been thrown out of Brownies and never made it to Girl Scouts.

"I guess I remember that," she said. "What did they throw me out for?"

"Swearing at Angela Carriman's mother." Jill grabbed the marshmallows. "We were in first grade."

Two houses away, someone dragged a plastic trash bin to the curb. Otherwise it was quiet. The stars began glittering overhead.

"We're going to be juniors this year," Jill said. "I used to think I'd feel old when I was a junior." She tossed a marshmallow into her mouth. "But I feel the same."

I felt the same, too. Maybe I would never feel older or more mature. When I tried to picture myself at forty or fifty or even eighty, all I could imagine was a gray-haired, confused-looking person sitting on a roof with her mouth full of food.

"I should go home now," Wallis said.

"You can't leave until we see a meteor," CeeCee told her.

Jill said that seemed fair.

In a month, I thought, Wallis would be living somewhere in Connecticut, I would be hanging out with Liz, Jill would be running half a dozen organizations, and CeeCee would rediscover how important she was and would probably pretend not to see me when we met in the hall.

CeeCee reached across me for the marshmallow bag. "Here's an epiphany," she said. "I think when you're older you should hire a detective to track down your dad. And when you find him, even if he's eighty years old and drooling into his soup, you should make him feel like crap for missing your childhood. You should tell him how incredibly fun every single second of it was."

"I don't think her childhood's been that much fun, though," Jill said. She licked some marshmallow dust from her fingers.

"It's starting to get cloudy," Wallis said. "That's why we aren't seeing meteors."

"We can't give up yet," CeeCee said. "We'll just have to kill a little time." She turned on the flashlight and gave it to me.

I asked if she expected me to use it to find a meteor.

"No." She handed me *The Awakening.*

"You don't want me to read out loud up here," I said. But she apparently did.

"I don't mind," Jill said. "My parents will probably be making out for another hour."

Wallis was frowning up at the sky.

"Go ahead. We're waiting," CeeCee said.

"Just don't read the ending, because I haven't gotten there yet." Jill popped a marshmallow into her mouth and lay down.

I opened the book, embarrassed but wishing that Ms. Radcliffe could see us, her AP English students on a roof in the dark, eating marshmallows and reading literature under the stars.

Wallis and Jill and I gave a brief summary of the plot for CeeCee: Edna Pontellier didn't love her husband—and seemed only occasionally interested in her kids—so she had spent her summer flirting with another man. Edna had thought she was one sort of person, but it turned out that she was someone else.

"A slut," Jill said.

"I don't think she's a slut," I said. "She's married."

"Can't married people be sluts?" Jill asked.

Wallis suggested that I read the part where Edna learns how to swim.

I flipped through the pages until I found it. I read about Edna's fear of the water and her first clumsy strokes. *"A feeling of exultation overtook her,"* I read, *"as if some power of significant import had been given to her."*

CeeCee lay still. Jill had stopped chewing. Wallis, though she was supposed to be looking for meteors, had shut her eyes. Edna *"grew daring and reckless,"* I read. She swam by herself, away from shore. *"A quick vision of death smote her soul."* But she finally staggered out of the water; she had learned how to swim.

"I definitely get a bad feeling about where this book is going," Jill said.

CeeCee stretched. She said that most of the books we read for school ended with someone dying, because teachers liked it when their students got depressed.

I read another page. *"'A thousand emotions have swept through me tonight,' Edna explained. 'I don't comprehend half of them.'"*

"I wish Edna would stay with her husband," Jill said. "I hate the guy she hooks up with. He's a total weasel."

I read another two pages and then stopped at the end of a paragraph. Wallis stood up. "I need to go home." It was fully dark.

"Take the flashlight with you," I said, wanting to be generous. I held it out to her but our hands collided, and the flashlight rolled down the slope of the roof and landed in the gutter with a metallic clunk.

"That's okay. I brought the headlamp your mother gave me," Wallis said. She pulled the elastic band from her pocket.

"You can SOS us," CeeCee said.

I asked if Wallis would be afraid by herself.

"No," she said. "What would I be afraid of?"

"I don't know. The dark. Evil people. Monsters. Thieves."

"I don't have anything a thief would want," Wallis said. "And the monsters don't notice me."

We took turns climbing back through the window into the attic and, bumping into each other, we navigated our way through the rest of the house. Wallis strapped the headlamp to her head. We walked her to the door.

"Where in Connecticut are you going to live?" CeeCee asked. "I have a cousin in Hartford."

"We'll be in a small town," Wallis said.

We stood on the porch, looking into the yard. It was one of those moments that in real life is probably short, but it stretched itself out, Wallis's hand reaching behind her for the metal latch on the door. One day we would read about her, I thought, when she discovered a new planet or a cure for cancer, and we would see her picture on TV or in the paper (by then she would probably wear her hair in a bun and have glamorous glasses) and I would wish I had found a way to tell her that we should keep in touch; that was what I was thinking, that I had to extend the moment before she opened the door and walked out of our unbearable book club and into the dark, and then Jill leaned forward to hug Wallis goodbye while at the very same moment CeeCee suggested that—even though none of us were supposed to be out; in fact, she herself was actually grounded for the first time in her life—she and Jill and I, for old times' sake and because it was our last evening together, should walk Wallis home.

• • • • • • • • • • •

17. CLIMAX: A climax is the high point or exciting part of something. Which doesn't mean it's necessarily good. Terrible things can happen during a climax. That's what I learned the night CeeCee and Jill and I walked Wallis home.

Every step we took that night brought us closer to a bad idea.

I looked back at my house, receding behind us. I pictured my mother coming home and finding the attic window open, a candle and some massacred hot dogs on the kitchen table, and a trail of spilled marshmallows leading to the roof.

But we couldn't let Wallis walk home by herself—which was why the four of us headed into the darkness under the trees, every light in West New Hope extinguished because of the storm.

"Your headlight's dying," Jill said as the oval light from Wallis's headlamp shivered and dimmed.

"Let me see it." CeeCee took the elastic strap from Wallis's head and shook it, then tapped the headlamp several times against the ground. The light went out completely.

"Well done," Jill said. She walked ahead of us. We were all moving slowly because of the fallen branches; leaves that should have dangled above us erupted, strangely, out of the ground.

Now that we were moving instead of sitting still, a piece of my epiphany started to come back to me. This was my chance to talk to Wallis. This was my chance to understand what her story was. I did have a theory: she and her mother were in hiding. That was why they were moving; it was why they had changed their last name and why Wallis's mother never went anywhere and never showed up at book club. That was why Wallis didn't want her picture taken and why they lived in an unnumbered house on Weller Road—they didn't want their stalker to know where they lived—and that was why Wallis's mother had (possibly) carried a gun. All I had to do was lay out the theory and say, "Is that right?"

But I didn't do it. Wallis would probably tell me that they weren't hiding: that her mother had gotten a job and they had changed their last name because her parents had gotten divorced. And she would say that they lived in an unnumbered house because they liked the quiet and that she had gotten a scar on her forehead because she fell down.

Jill asked how my leg was holding up; I said it was fine.

We walked through the playground: three cement tubes

to crawl through, a slide that led to a pile of foul-smelling sand, and four rusted swings. We walked past the road that led to Jill's. But it was only when we crossed the soccer field that I understood where we were going. We didn't have to walk past it on the way to Wallis's, but maybe out of habit, or maybe because we sensed that, like the heart-shaped pointer on Jill's Ouija board, it might have the ability to tell us something, we ended up at the pool.

With the lights off, at night, something about the fence and the trees around it looked very different. There was the spot where we usually sat; there were the diving board and the lifeguard chair; there was the gate near the locker rooms. And around the corner behind the locker rooms, there was something else.

CeeCee put her hand on the chain link and followed the path around the fence.

"*Un*believable," she said. And it almost was.

A tree had fallen. Its roots had torn themselves out of the earth, clutching several large rocks in their wooden fingers. As if it knew we were coming, the tree had fallen directly onto the fence, which had crumpled at the top like a piece of tinfoil.

"This is a black walnut tree," Wallis said as CeeCee pulled experimentally on one of the branches.

"Don't," Jill said. "I know what you're thinking. And we're not going to do it."

CeeCee turned toward her. "Do you wear your seat belt at the dinner table?" she asked. She backed up toward the tangled roots of the tree, then leaned her weight against

208

the trunk. "It's totally stuck," she said. "Feel it. It's not going to budge."

The trunk was at least a foot in diameter. The branches were caught on both sides of the fence, which kept the whole tree still. It was a rounded balance beam with handholds.

Jill reminded me that I didn't want to hurt my leg. "I'll lose my job if anyone sees us."

"It's August," I told her. The tree seemed to have laid down its life for our benefit. "How much longer were you going to work?"

CeeCee was already halfway up the trunk. I could barely see her; she had been swallowed up in the foliage.

"If this is fate, I don't like the looks of it," Jill said. "We'll jump in and then out, CeeCee," she called.

"Whatever you say," CeeCee agreed. "Wallis, are you coming? We're finally going to teach you to swim."

Walking up the ridged, uneven slope of the walnut tree, I understood that we should have turned around and gone home. But it felt like the crucial moment that our entire summer had been leading up to: the moment when the four key members of the Literary Trespassers Association for Delinquent Girls would climb over a locked chain-link fence during a blackout to get back to the place where everything had started: the pool.

Wallis was in front of me, her flat feet gripping the tree trunk in a simian way.

"I'm going to be fired tomorrow," Jill said, for the third or fourth time.

I grabbed the next branch, looking down at the crinkled fence below. A few more steps, and the four of us stood on the tar-paper roof of the locker room. Jill muttered something about juvenile court and about how CeeCee was going to look in her orange road-crew vest, picking up trash along the highway. But she was the one who pointed out the branch that led to the stack of reclining chairs; she was the first one to kick off her shoes on the way to the pool. "Let's hurry up if we're going to do this," she said.

CeeCee took off her shirt and unbuttoned her jeans. I couldn't help noticing that her bra and her underwear matched.

"Watch and learn, Wallis." She walked to the edge, near the NO DIVING sign, and neatly dived in.

I felt like a person under a spell. The water looked like a blank page on which we had been invited to inscribe ourselves.

Jill took off her shorts and dropped them by the lifeguard's chair. She hung her shirt over one of its rungs. "Wallis, you have to stay at the shallow end," she said. Then she followed CeeCee, who had resurfaced, into the pool.

Something graceful and dark—a swallow or a bat—swooped over the water.

Trying not to think about the underwear I had put on that morning, I took off my shirt and then my shorts and quickly groped my way down the ladder. I kept a close eye on Wallis, who had taken off her shorts but kept her shirt on. She clutched the ladder and came step by step into the shallow end. I saw her take off her glasses and set them carefully at the edge of the pool.

"Lesson one," CeeCee said, swimming toward Wallis. "You have to learn how to float. Lie on your back." She held a hand under Wallis's rib cage, but every time she took it away, Wallis sank. "Your bones must be made out of lead," CeeCee told her. "Take a breath. You have to fill yourself with air."

Wallis opened her mouth in an O, breathed in, and then clamped her lips and eyes tightly shut. I could hear CeeCee laugh. Wallis threw her arms out to the sides and lay down on the water; five seconds later, one inch at a time, she began to submerge.

"Taking a breath like that, you should be unsinkable," CeeCee said. She hauled Wallis up.

"That's why I haven't learned," Wallis said. "I always sink." She wiped her eyes.

Jill and I tried to teach her by having her stand in waist-deep water, turning her head from side to side, and paddling her arms. She looked like a circus animal practicing a strange new trick. I think all four of us were happy at that exact moment. I held the back of Wallis's shirt while she tried to paddle, still sinking, between CeeCee and Jill.

We were going to leave as soon as we went a little bit deeper, just to the middle of the pool, so Wallis could share the feeling of being almost weightless. We held her up, our eight legs flashing, pale, like reeds in the water.

Jill saw him first. "Shit," she said.

All I saw was a shape running toward us. I gave Wallis a shove in the direction of the shallow end.

"I'm getting my phone," CeeCee said, but then the

211

shape came to a sudden stop at the edge of the pool: it was Jeff.

"You jerk. You scared us," CeeCee said.

He peeled off his shirt and cannonballed into the water.

"Let's go," Jill said. "It's time to leave."

CeeCee started to get out of the pool but Jeff grabbed her ankle. "I didn't think anything scared CeeCee Christiansen," he said. "You don't need to go. You haven't finished your striptease."

"You're drunk," CeeCee said. "Drunk and disgusting." She splashed him and dived under the water; when she surfaced, Jeff dunked her.

She spluttered and coughed. "Don't touch me," she said.

Jeff laughed. He said a few things I won't repeat here.

"Is he the one who emailed our pictures?" Wallis asked.

Jeff spun around in the water. "Maybe *you* want to finish the striptease."

"Leave her alone." CeeCee grabbed at his leg. Jeff lunged at her and dunked her again.

All over the inside of the fence around the pool, clearly printed signs warned swimmers that there was NO RUNNING NO CLIMBING ON LIFEGUARD CHAIRS NO HORSEPLAY NO TALKING TO GUARDS.

"You think you're strong?" Jeff asked. He pulled CeeCee in the direction of the diving board. "Show me how strong you are."

CeeCee was thrashing; I heard her swear.

"Where are the life preservers?" Jill asked. She got out of the pool and ran toward the fence.

NO DIVING AT THIS END, the signs warned. SAFETY FIRST

"Get the hell off me!" CeeCee yelled.

I wasn't sure whether I should help her or stay with Wallis.

Lights were coming toward us from the main road. "It's a car," I said, and for the first time, it occurred to me that getting out—climbing back up the stack of recliners and the dangling branch to get to the locker room's roof— would be much harder than getting in.

"Come on!" Jill was shouting. "CeeCee, let's go."

I heard someone coughing.

"I can't find my glasses," Wallis said. She was behind me; we were both getting out of the water. I felt something bump against my leg.

The headlight beams were gliding across the chain-link fence.

I wanted to find my clothes; Jill told me to forget them. We ran.

We ran past the lifeguard stands and across the shuffle-board court and around the baby pool (I heard someone stumbling heavily through it), then around the deck chairs by the crumpled fence (there was no way that, without help, I would be able to climb it), under the awning where Jill had sold Italian water ice and soda and ice cream, and into the mildewed cavern of the girls' locker room.

I rammed my knee into a bench.

"Quiet," somebody said.

I stuffed my wrist into my mouth to keep from shouting because of the pain. I crawled to the back of the shower

213

room, which was as dark as a dungeon—the darkness was a warm black cloth held in front of my eyes.

"I don't want to be arrested half naked." Jill's whispered voice came from the opposite side of the room. "I'm going to find something to wear in the lost and found."

I heard a soft scuffling. I imagined what my mother would say when she saw me in the back of a police car. The air smelled of chlorine and moldy flip-flops. "Here's a towel, I think," Jill said.

I thought about Edna Pontellier, in her muslin gown, walking down to the water.

"And this might be a shirt." Jill was still rustling through the lost and found. Was someone breathing behind me? "I think Adrienne fell in the baby pool," Jill said.

"I didn't fall." We weren't whispering anymore. I was clutching my knee. The car seemed to have gone.

"Where are you?" Jill asked.

"I'm right over here."

She threw me a shirt and I put it on. "CeeCee, where are you?"

"Behind you." CeeCee sighed. "I can't believe Jeff showed up. What a jackass."

"Then it must have been Wallis who fell," Jill said.

I remembered Wallis's glasses, bumping into my leg on their way to the bottom of the pool. But Wallis and I were both in the shallow end. "Wallis?" I asked. "Are you in here?"

The darkness was thick. Edna Pontellier entered the water.

"Wallis?"

214

18. RESOLUTION: The part of the book you spend a lot of pages waiting for; the part where you get your questions answered. (But I'm not sure if that's true in my essay.)

"I am very sorry to hear about the death of your friend," Dr. Ramsan said. He'd read the article in the paper, which had mentioned my name. "It is a terrible thing when a young person dies."

My knee was back in its brace, and I was back in Dr. Ramsan's office, as if it were the beginning of the summer instead of almost the end.

"Please sit at the center of the table," he said.

I sat. I took off my brace. Meanwhile my mind, like a private theater with a crazed projectionist, began to play its favorite film from the Extremely Unbearable Book Club Meeting #5, our last night at the pool. I saw CeeCee, in her underwear, running out of the locker room in front of me, and Jill crashing into a mountain of deck chairs, both of them illuminated by the sudden appearance of a quarter moon. Limping behind them, I already knew, as if I had memorized the details in a photograph, what we would see when we reached the water: the glassy surface gone still again, and imprisoned within it, Wallis, facedown, one hand gesturing toward the glasses that were just out of reach.

I closed my eyes.

"Can you straighten your leg?" Dr. Ramsan asked.

Jill had called me on the morning of the funeral. "We're idiots," she said. "We should never have gone into the pool. Or climbed the fence. We should have stayed home."

"Now bend your leg," Dr. Ramsan said. "Good. Like that."

I had tried to hang up, but Jill wouldn't let me. She needed to call us both some more names. "And there's something else I have to tell you." Her mother had found the missing pills. She'd been cleaning the bathroom, and something had rattled up the nozzle of her vacuum cleaner, stopping the hose. When she took the vacuum apart and found the small plastic bottle, she had shouted for Jill, and they both sat on the bathroom floor and cried. "They were here in our house the whole time," Jill said. "They must have fallen out of the cabinet." She asked me if I was wearing black to the funeral.

In the film in my head, which ran even when my eyes were tightly closed, Wallis's glasses continued bumping along the bottom of the pool as if pulled by a string. Jill called an ambulance, which seemed to take forever to reach us. I hadn't heard the siren because I was kneeling on the cement, the scar on my leg torn open; I was trying

216

to talk myself through the steps I had paid attention to only casually when we learned them at school: *tilt the head back, pinch the nose shut; one–one thousand, two–one thousand . . .* Eventually, a paramedic pulled me aside, and only then did I become aware of the blood, and the red and blue lights revolving and flashing outside the gate.

"Does this hurt?" Dr. Ramsan asked.

One of the paramedics asked me some questions but I was confused and didn't answer.

"And this? Does it hurt?" Dr. Ramsan asked.

"Yes," I said.

He let go of my leg and put his arm around my shoulders. "Such a painful and difficult thing. The parts of our lives that don't yet make sense to us," he said. "There is always hope that we will understand them."

He handed me a tissue and bowed his head while I blew my nose. Then he handed me my brace, and I put it on while he typed up his notes. "Are you still a member of a book club?" he asked. He looked at the keyboard while he typed.

"No, that's over now," I said. "It was just for the summer."

"Ah. That's too bad. I was hoping you would recommend something for me. I enjoyed the Le Guin."

"You read it?" I asked.

"On your recommendation—of course." He was typing with only three of his fingers. "Books are a distraction but also a comfort. Don't you agree?"

"I guess so," I said.

He finished typing, then folded his stethoscope into

his jacket pocket, embroidered with bright blue letters: *V. Ramsan, MD*. He stood up. "Again, my deepest condolences on the death of your friend."

"Thanks," I said. "But—we weren't friends."

Dr. Ramsan paused in the doorway and tugged at his beard.

"The article in the paper made it sound like we were." I stepped down, carefully, from the table. "But I barely knew him," I said. "He dated the sister of a friend of mine. His name was Jeff."

The ending of a good book, I had always thought—at least, a book that sticks with you—should be satisfying but also sad. A character should die, or almost die, and the people left behind should see things differently. They should change.

And the final pages of a book should suggest that, even though difficult and ugly and unexpected things happen, they happen within a pattern or a framework, and can be understood. They might seem random, but the reader will be able to find meaning in them. Believing in books, I thought, was almost like believing in God.

In real life, though, the details didn't always add up. I didn't generally get the feeling that an author was pointing to the relevant parts of my life with an enormous, omniscient finger, connecting the dots between a novel written in the 1800s, a fallen tree, and a pair of glasses spilled at night into a swimming pool. Jeff had probably tripped, the police decided. He was drunk and had suffered a "significant blow to the head," drowning in water (the baby pool) that barely covered his ankles. He was so heavy. And it was so hard to turn him over and get him out of the water. I was afraid to look at the gash above his eyebrow. There was blood on the cement and more blood in the pool.

Jill ran for her phone while CeeCee grabbed a towel and pressed it to Jeff's head to stop the bleeding. She was shouting at me to do something, but I was already kneeling beside him with my hands on his chest. Was his heart still beating? I pinched his nose shut, feeling my own heart pounding against my ribs. Then I covered Jeff's mouth with mine the way CeeCee had always told me I would. His eyes were half open, and his skin, maybe from the temperature of the water, was cool.

I had almost forgotten about Wallis, but when I turned my head, putting my ear on Jeff's chest to listen for a heartbeat, I saw her coming out of the boys' locker room. *One–one thousand, two–one thousand.* She was wearing her glasses. She must have run through the wrong doorway, I thought. It was understandable: she hadn't been to the pool as often as we had, and she had probably lost track of us as we were running toward the locker room in the dark.

The pool closed for the summer. It would take several days to clear away the fallen tree and fix the fence; and the water would have to be drained because of the blood.

Jill said she would have quit her job anyway. "I don't ever want to swim in that pool again," she said. After the funeral she went to visit her grandparents in Virginia. Meanwhile, CeeCee and her parents left for two weeks in Paris. (I got a single short text from her: *Au revoir.*)

My mother and I stayed in West New Hope. She took several days off during the week of the funeral, saying that she didn't want me to be alone. But I avoided her when I could. I sat on the porch, refusing her offers to play Scrabble (I didn't need the humiliation) or to take a bike ride (my knee hurt) or to talk.

It wasn't like her to hover, but she was definitely hovering.

"I guess you heard that Wallis and her mother are leaving town," she said, lingering in the doorway of the porch.

I said I had heard.

"Apparently, her mother finished writing her book. It's called *A Study of Existence*. With a long subtitle. Maybe we'll buy a copy and read it."

I couldn't imagine reading a book called *A Study of Existence*. It would probably just take up space on our shelves. There were so many other books to read, anyway, because at that very moment people in coffee shops and at kitchen tables and on buses all over the world were linking phrases and sentences together like boxcars and shipping them off to be published.

"Liz will be back next week, won't she?" my mother asked.

"Thursday," I said.

My mother dusted the surface of the table with her hand, then sat down next to me on the wicker couch. The problem with wicker: bugs and dirt were always stuck in its crevices. I poked at a grimy spot on the armrest.

"Adrienne," my mother said. "You might feel better if you talked about it."

I pulled at a thread on the hem of my shirt. What was there to say? I was in a mother-daughter book club that killed a person.

"I'm sure all four of you are having a difficult time," she said. "It's going to be hard for quite a while." A breeze cut through the screens above our heads. "But I want you to know that I felt proud of you when"—my mother stopped and took a breath—"when I found out how hard you tried to save him."

"Don't," I said.

"Nine minutes," my mother said. "You tried to breathe for him for nine minutes, until the paramedics got there."

"It didn't work, though," I said. I leaned against her.

"He was under the water too long," she said. "But you tried. You kept your wits about you. I think that was heroic."

"It wasn't," I said. I was not heroic. I was not a heroine. I tugged at the loose thread on my shirt. "It wasn't the ending I wanted."

"No." My mother took my hand away from the thread I was pulling. "I don't want you unraveling," she said.

We sat on the wicker couch for a while. My mother suggested that we order a pizza, and I agreed that we should. But neither one of us moved.

I didn't intend to tell her the entire story. I just wanted to tell her one thing: what Jeff had looked like—helpless and lost, with his head thrown back—when we managed to drag him out of the pool. But then I ended up telling her about the first time I'd met him, about how he'd shown up with CeeCee that night at my bedroom window. I told

221

her about CeeCee piercing my ear in a moving car while Jeff drove us both to the mini-putt, and then I told her about the night I'd gotten drunk on the way to Wallis's, and about Jeff (who had started to seem like a nicer person, now that I was describing him) driving me to CeeCee's after I fell from the tower. I told her I had seen Wallis and her mother that night, and I had talked to Dr. Ramsan about hallucinations. I told her CeeCee was dyslexic, which was probably why our relationship started, because she had asked me to read to her from *Frankenstein*. My mother didn't interrupt or ask questions, so I didn't stop; I was a flood of words moving downhill. I told her about the blog and about Wallis's picture, and about how I had jumped to conclusions because I thought I'd seen a gun. I described Wallis's scar. I told her about CeeCee telling me I should find out who my father was, and about Jill's parents picking her out of a lineup of babies, as one in a million. And because she still didn't stop me or interrupt, I told my mother I hated our question-and-answer sessions and I'd read my aunt Beatrice's email, and though I'd always known that no one had planned on me or wanted me, I never used to think of myself as a mistake—but I obviously was one. I told her Jill knew she wanted to be a nurse and Wallis was already a genius and CeeCee would probably become a millionaire in Paris and Liz would soon be coming home to West New Hope having transformed herself into an expert in all things outdoors—but I would be . . . nothing. I was the only person on the planet who walked through the world all day feeling incomplete. I wanted to be smart and to be a serious person, but I was impressionable and susceptible and absurd, and I knew my mother would never be proud of me because I couldn't make sense of things the way people did in books; and I felt terrible about Jeff and I was sorry about everything I had ruined, but I had just wanted to be part of a story; I wanted to be a person who had a story to tell.

My mother waited until I was finished. Then she lifted her feet off the floor and moved the pillows around on the couch and gently nudged me aside with her hip so we were both lying down. She said, "You were not a mistake." Then she said it again. "You are not a mistake. I have always loved you. And you are not a person without a story. You are Adrienne Haus."

I pushed my face into the crook of her neck. "We shouldn't have gone to the pool," I said.

We lay still without talking for a while.

My mother said, "I'm sorry about the question-and-answer sessions. We'll find a better way to communicate."

I couldn't speak. I had run out of words.

"And I know what you mean about feeling incomplete," she said. "I feel that way sometimes. Restless, I guess. I feel like I'm searching. As if I'm groping around in the dark. But usually, the thing I'm looking for is right here."

"What's the thing you're looking for?" I asked.

Our feet were touching. My feet were bigger than hers, I noticed. But they had the same shape, the second toe longer than the first.

My mother said, "You."

19. EPILOGUE: The last part of a book, kind of like a PS that might hint at the future of the characters.

That night after dinner, I took *The Awakening* out to the porch. I suspected things weren't going to end very well for Edna, but it seemed only fair that I see her story through. The overhead light turned the pages yellow. Cicadas hurled their knobby bodies against the screens.

My mother had taken a plate of brownies to our neighbors, who had just tied a cluster of blue balloons to their mailbox that announced: IT'S A BOY! She'd been gone about fifteen minutes when, turning the final page of the book, I saw a small white truck pull in the drive.

Wallis got out on the passenger side. She saw me on the porch and walked up the back sidewalk.

"I thought you left town already," I said, getting up.

"We're leaving now. I came to return these to you." She held out copies of *The Left Hand of Darkness* and *The Awakening*.

I opened the screen door and stepped out. Looking past her, I could see that the white truck was packed with boxes. Wallis's mother (that had to be her mother, didn't it?) was behind the wheel. I waved to her as if to say, *No hard feelings about my being drunk at your house that night and thinking you were insane,* but she was wearing oversized dark glasses and didn't seem to be looking in my direction.

"Did you finish *The Awakening*?" I asked Wallis.

She said she had. "Tell your mother thanks for the books." She turned to leave.

"It was a weird coincidence, wasn't it?" I asked. "What happened in the book and what happened to Jeff? I know it was an accident."

"I have to go," Wallis said. The truck's motor was running.

I didn't want her to leave. "I keep going over it in my head," I told her. "If he hadn't been drunk, or if we hadn't panicked and run when we saw the headlights—"

Wallis blinked. The lens in one side of her glasses was scratched.

"He was running behind us," I said. "And I realized later that he must have tripped over my shoes. I left my shoes in front of the baby pool and he probably tripped on them and that's why he's dead. You're the only person I've told."

"I need to get going," Wallis said.

"Right. Okay." Feeling awkward, I patted her arm. "I hope things go well for you in Connecticut. I hope you find another book club."

She started walking away.

"I'm sorry I wasn't a nicer person to you, Wallis," I said. "I'm sorry I imagined things about you that weren't true."

She had reached the driveway but turned around. "He didn't trip over your shoes," she said. She scratched her leg. "He tripped over one of the life preservers."

I watched her climb up into the truck. When she closed the door, I said, as if to myself, "But we didn't see him fall. We were already in the locker room. If we had seen him trip and fall—" Wallis didn't look in my direction when they drove away.

My mother got back about twenty minutes later. "New babies smell wonderful," she said. "Did you finish the book?"

I said that I had, and we talked about Edna Pontellier for a little while. We agreed that the other characters in the novel had wanted to script her life for her, when what she wanted was the chance to write it herself.

We saw a flash of orange and heard a terrified squeal in the bushes.

"There won't be a living bird or chipmunk left within a hundred yards of this house by the end of August," my mother said. She saw the books Wallis had returned. "Did they stop by while I was gone?" she asked.

I said that they had.

"It's too bad they needed to leave town," my mother said. "I wonder what sort of job her mother got in Utah."

"They went to Connecticut," I said.

"No, her mother definitely said Utah," my mother said. "I spoke to her at the funeral."

"She was there?" I asked.

"At the back of the church, all by herself," my mother said. "I offered to bring them dinner while they were packing, but she said no. She was a bit . . . eccentric. Skittish." She stacked "The Yellow Wallpaper" and *Frankenstein* and *The Left Hand of Darkness* and *The House on Mango Street* and *The Awakening* on top of each other.

I looked at the driveway where the truck had been.

"Let's read one final book together," my mother said. "Just you and me. Maybe something by Jane Austen this time. *Pride and Prejudice*? Or *Northanger Abbey*?"

"Next summer," I said.

I straightened the books on the table between us. Edna and Esperanza and Genly and Frankenstein's monster and the crazy woman in the yellow room: it seemed they all wanted to tell me something. They wanted to talk to me about this person named Adrienne Haus. They wanted Adrienne to tell them a story about the things that had happened to her over the summer.

I opened my laptop.

"What are you doing?" my mother asked.

"I have an idea for that essay I have to write," I said.

BIBLIOGRAPHY

Chopin, Kate. *The Awakening and Selected Stories of Kate Chopin,* Barbara H. Solomon, editor. New York: Signet Classics/New American Library, 1976.

This book is about Edna Pontellier, who lived near New Orleans, where it was incredibly hot (like West New Hope in the summer). Maybe because she got annoyed with her husband, who *was* pretty annoying, she flirted with Robert and then slept with Arobin, who was a total weasel.

Cisneros, Sandra. *The House on Mango Street.* New York: Vintage Books, 1989.

This is the newest of the books we read. If you're a girl reading this book, you're obviously supposed to identify with the narrator, Esperanza, but I identified more with Genly Ai in *The Left Hand of Darkness.* This book is written in tiny pieces, as if somebody took it outside, put it on a rock, and smacked it with a hammer.

Gilman, Charlotte Perkins. "The Yellow Wallpaper." Wilder Publications, 2011.

I'm glad everybody in class had to read this book. In fact, if there were a list of books that every single person on the planet had to read, I think this should be on it. "The Yellow Wallpaper" is about a person who is going crazy because her husband thinks he knows what is best for her. Maybe that's the lesson we're supposed to take from all of these books: you have to think for yourself. (On the other hand, I don't think books should make you feel like you're learning lessons.)

Le Guin, Ursula K. *The Left Hand of Darkness*. New York: Ace Science Fiction Books, 1986.

Even at the beginning of this book when he is uptight and a bit of a jerk, I really liked Genly. I liked Estraven, too. I liked the way that at first they seemed to be enemies, but gradually they got closer. My mother says that some books are good no matter when you read them, and some are good at a particular moment; they come into your life at just the right time.

Shelley, Mary. *Frankenstein or The Modern Prometheus*. Oxford, England: Oxford University Press, 1986.

Frankenstein is a book about a nameless monster. Everybody thinks the monster's name is Frankenstein, but that's actually the name of the guy who sews him together. I think if the monster were alive today, and he had to sit in the audience (I picture him wearing a really nice tux), clapping and smiling while his creator got all the credit, he would be pissed off.

ACKNOWLEDGMENTS

Many thanks to my agent, Lisa Bankoff, for her steadfast support, and to my editors at Delacorte Press, Michelle Poploff and Rebecca Short, for their gracious hands-on expertise.

Thanks to Kate DiCamillo for her kindness and encouragement during moments of doubt, to Swati Avasthi for her generosity and insight, and to Mary François Rockcastle for that hilarious weekend at the cabin.

Thanks to the members of the many groups of which I have been a part: the book club (now in its twenty-second year!), the WWW writers' group, the lacrosse team, the basketball league, and JWIRL. Even when books are not directly involved, I do appreciate being invited into a group.